THE SHADOW
OF THE
SHIFTING SANDS

Wendy Leighton-Porter

Published by Silver Quill Publishing 2025

Written in English (UK)

ISBN 978-1-912513-11-6

Silver Quill Publishing

The Shadow of the Shifting Sands

Silver Quill Publishing
2025

"A fantastic addition to the *Shadows of the Past* series. It's the perfect book for middle-grade fantasy enthusiasts who love time-travel adventure tales. From talking animals to young heroes embarking on courageous quests seeking ancient cities, this book has it all. The intricately crafted plot will keep you hooked from beginning to end. Preteen readers will find a lot to love about this series as a whole."
READERS' FAVORITE Book Reviews

"A captivating time-travel adventure that unfolds like a desert mirage full of mystery, danger, and buried secrets."
ALL AUTHOR

"The latest Shadows of the Past story is a real page-turner and worthy of being made into a film or a cartoon. I've read and reviewed all the books in the series, but The Shadow of the Shifting Sands is one of my favourites and I will definitely read it again."
IONA CARROLL, author of the *Oisin Kelly* series

"Another gripping '*Shadows*' read. The Lancelot twins, with Max and friend Charlie, find themselves in the Arabian desert where they are chased by pirates eager to get their hands on a mystical pearl. Truly atmospheric and imaginative!"
OLIVER EADE, author

"*The Shadow of the Shifting Sands* takes Max the time-travelling cat back again to the Arabian desert... and, with his return, ancient spirits are awakened. Be prepared for non-stop adventure as the four travel into the perilous Empty Quarter."
CHERYL CARPINELLO, author of Children's, Middle Grade and Young Adult fiction

Also by Wendy Leighton-Porter

The Shadow of Atlantis
The Shadow of the Minotaur
The Shadow of the Trojan Horse
The Shadow of the Pyramid
The Shadow of the Volcano
The Shadow of Camelot
The Shadow of the Norman Arrow
Max's Arabian Adventure
Max's Christmas Adventure
The Shadow of the Two Princes
Max's Midnight Adventure
Max's Undercover Adventure
The Shadow of the Tudor Rose
Max's Hallowe'en Adventure
The Shadow of the Witchfinder
Max's Royal Adventure
The Shadow of the Great Fire
Max's Diary – Tales of a Time-travelling Cat

Find out more:
www.wendy-leighton-porter.com

SHADOWS OF THE PAST

This is the 18th adventure in the series, but if you haven't read any of the others, you might find it helpful to know a little of what has gone before.

Shadows of the Past is the title of an old book belonging to James Lancelot, a dealer in ancient texts and manuscripts. James had been keen to acquire it because he'd heard rumours of its magical properties. He was right, for this was no ordinary book but a gateway into the past, a portal that could transport you into the pages of history. Kept securely in a wooden chest, along with the magical book, was a key that enabled time-travellers to unlock its secrets but, more importantly, to return to the present after their travels.

Disaster strikes when James and his wife Isabel set off on one of their journeys into the past. They make a terrible mistake, forgetting to take the key with them, and are now trapped, lost somewhere in the mists of time, unable to return home. No one knows where they've gone or what's happened to them... apart from Max, the family cat, the sole witness to their disappearance. The couple vanished without a trace, leaving behind their children, 10-year-old twins, Jemima and Joe.

With their parents missing, the twins are sent to live with their father's brother, Richard Lancelot, a professor of ancient history and archaeology at the University of London. It's a tough time for them, until they meet a new friend, their next-door neighbour Charlie.

One day, the youngsters come across the old book amongst their parents' possessions and, before long, they discover its secrets for themselves, for Jemima has inherited her mother's necklace with the all-important key. However, the children find something else that James had missed, hidden in a secret compartment in the base of the wooden chest – four golden owl charms which give the wearer the power to speak and understand any language, both human and animal. When they attach the fourth charm to Max's collar, they are astounded to hear the cat speak, and he now tells them the truth about their parents' disappearance.

Knowing their parents are simply lost somewhere in the pages of history sparks a quest to find them and so the children's adventures begin. Travelling into the past, they visit famous moments in history, myth, and legend as they follow the trail through a series of events that have cast a shadow for one reason or another. Starting in the ancient city of Atlantis, each journey moves forward in time, taking them one step closer to what they seek.

However, it soon becomes clear that there's another reason for all of this and a startling truth emerges. The children's footsteps are being guided by the Guardians of Time, a mysterious group who send their specially trained agents back into the past in an attempt to put right the wrongdoings of mankind, to give people a second chance, and the opportunity to rewrite history.

But that's not all: Max, the large and handsome Tonkinese cat, quickly takes centre stage and, with each passing adventure, he becomes increasingly crucial to the success of their expeditions into the past. It also becomes apparent that Max's destiny was fixed from the time he was born. A collision between two stars in the constellation of Leo resulted in magical stardust falling upon him at the moment of his birth. The Guardians even take him to their secret training academy where, under the code name of *009 Lives*, Max achieves Special Agent status to prepare him for the rest of his missions, some of which he must accomplish alone.

For my dear girls,
Sheikha Shamma and Hind

Ancient secrets lie hidden beneath
the shifting sands of time...

Prologue

Arabia, 1700

The sun was just beginning to set over the endless stretch of golden sand, casting a fiery glow across the tranquil waters of the Arabian Gulf. The air smelled of salt and the promise of adventure. Zayed, a ten-year-old boy, sat in the wooden dhow with his father, feeling the small boat rock as they drifted on the gentle swell of the waves.

Zayed loved pearl fishing. There was something magical about diving deep beneath the surface, feeling the cool embrace of the sea, and searching for the perfect pearl hidden in the depths. It was a family tradition passed down through generations, a tradition that Zayed felt proud to carry on.

His father, Khaled, was a seasoned pearl diver, his skin weathered by the sun and salt, his hands calloused from years of hard work. He was a quiet man, a man of few words, but his eyes sparkled whenever he spoke of his trade.

'You must have patience, Zayed,' his father told him as the young boy prepared for his last dive of the day. 'The sea gives only to those who wait and who are worthy of her treasures.'

With a nod, Zayed climbed over the side of the dhow and dropped into the water. He felt a strange tingle of anticipation as he began to sink, holding onto the heavy stone tied to the rope. It was almost as if he'd known that something unusual was going to happen – call it a premonition, if you like – but as soon as he spotted the massive oyster shell, lying partly open on the seabed, a shiver had run down his spine.

With only a small amount of precious air left in his burning lungs, Zayed prised the shell wide open with his bare fingers. Stunned to see the size of the pale pink pearl nestled inside, he clawed it out with his fingernails before popping it inside his *deyeen* – the woven bag hanging around his neck. He left the open, empty shell abandoned on the seabed.

With his last remaining breath, he tugged on the line and his father hauled him back up to the surface. The boy climbed onto the dhow, his chest heaving.

That oyster shell had been far larger than

any he'd ever seen before, and the pearl it contained was simply magnificent – huge and flawless. His fingers still tingled from the satin-smooth touch of it.

As Zayed got his breath back, his father coiled the line and the rope with the stone attached, moving them out of the way.

'I think we're done for today,' said Khaled, his voice calm as he watched the horizon. 'Have you recovered enough for us to make a move?'

Zayed nodded, his heart racing. He could feel the weight of the day's catch in the boat – dozens of oyster shells, some empty, some full of tiny pearls. But none of them big enough to make his heart race, like the one he'd just found, hidden deep on the seabed.

He took the pearl from the soft woven bag and held it out to his astonished father. 'Look at what I found, Baba.'

Khaled gasped, scarcely able to believe his eyes when he saw the enormous pearl cupped in Zayed's hands.

'I've never seen another one like this,' said Zayed, his eyes dancing with excitement at his find. 'It must be worth a fortune. We'll be rich – very rich – won't we, Baba? Imagine what it will mean for our family… our tribe.'

Khaled continued to stare at the iridescent pearl, which almost seemed to glow from within as it captured the sun's rays, and something stirred deep within him – a long-forgotten memory. As he reached out a trembling finger, he heard a loud splash. Turning to stare out to sea, his heart gave a sickening lurch.

From the distance, a dark shadow moved swiftly towards them. At first, Zayed thought it was a school of fish, but the shape grew larger and larger until he could make out the unmistakable silhouette of a ship. But not just any ship – a pirate ship, with tattered sails and a black flag flying high on its mast.

Before Zayed could even speak, his father's hand shot out, gripping his arm tightly. 'Get down!' Khaled whispered fiercely, pushing Zayed flat against the bottom of the boat.

The menacing shadow of the pirate ship loomed closer now, rapidly narrowing the gap with terrifying speed as it cut a deadly path through the waves.

Zayed heard the sound of shouting and the clink of metal. He could feel the heat rising in his chest as panic took hold of him.

'What are we going to do, Baba?' he asked in a quivering voice.

Khaled's face was hard, his eyes narrowed with fear, but his voice was steady. 'Don't make a sound, my son. They must not find that pearl. Keep it safe at all costs.'

In his haste to hide it from the men, Zayed fumbled with the strap of the *deyeen*, his fingers trembling as he tried to unfasten the knot holding it in place around his neck. Just in time, the knot came loose and he quickly shoved the woven bag under his tunic, retying the cord around his waist. The pearl was safely hidden from sight.

The pirate ship was nearly upon them now. Zayed could see the pirates – tall, fierce-looking men with curved swords at their sides and scowls on their faces. They'd spotted the small boat through their telescope and now their eyes were fixed on Khaled and Zayed, their intentions clear.

The pirates boarded the boat with ease, their bare feet thudding against the wood.

Zayed's heart pounded as he squeezed the pearl in the *deyeen* bag through the fabric of his tunic. Feeling its cool smoothness through the cloth, he knew he had to hold on to the pearl. He had to protect it.

One of the pirates, a man with a crooked nose and the tattoo of a cobra running down the side of his neck, towered over them. He grinned wickedly, revealing yellow teeth, as he tucked a small telescope into his belt.

'You two have something that belongs to us,' the pirate growled. His eyes flicked down to the boat's contents, scanning the pile of oysters and the fishing tools. 'You will give us everything.'

Zayed's pulse raced. He knew that the pirates were after their pearls, the precious treasures of the sea. But they didn't know about *his* pearl – the one hidden in the bag under his tunic... or *did* they?

Khaled stood tall, his chest rising with a deep breath. 'We have nothing of yours,' he said firmly.

The pirate's grin grew wider. 'I think you're lying, old man. Look around you – your boat tells a different story.'

Zayed felt his father stiffen beside him. He didn't know what would happen next, but he knew one thing – he had to save the pearl, whatever it took.

As the pirates began to tie his father up, Zayed knew what he must do. He had to escape. He had to find a way to get away from these men and stop them from taking the pearl.

In that moment, as the pirate with the snake tattoo turned his back, Zayed made his move. With a burst of energy, he scrambled free, darting across the boat with surprising speed. His heart pounded in his chest as he leapt over the side, diving into the water below without a second thought.

He swam away from the boat, staying underwater for as long as he could hold his breath before pushing his way back up to the surface, hoping he was far enough away by now.

Splashing through the waves, Zayed swam furiously towards the shore, his breath coming in ragged gasps. He didn't dare look back, didn't dare to see if the pirates were following him. All that mattered was reaching the safety of the beach – and keeping his beautiful pearl out of their thieving hands.

As he neared dry land, Zayed pushed harder until, at last, he reached the shallows. He stumbled onto the soft sand, his body shaking from exhaustion. He sank to his knees, his fingers trembling as he reached under his tunic for the woven bag. The pearl was still in there, gleaming softly in the fading light of the day.

He'd done it. He'd escaped. But what would happen next? Would the pirates come looking for him? And what about his father? What would they do to him if they suspected Zayed had taken any of that day's pearl harvest when he'd jumped ship?

He stood up, wiping the salt water from his face. He knew that his journey was far from over and there could still be many dangers ahead. But one thing was certain – he would not let anyone take the pearl, not without a fight. Not ever.

Zayed looked back out to sea, searching the horizon for the two boats, and saw their dark shapes silhouetted against the crimson light of the setting sun. As he watched, he thought the pirate ship appeared to be moving closer and knew he couldn't stay out there in the open, waiting for them to come and get him. Torn between not wanting to leave his father and the need to hide from the pirates, he came to a swift decision. After a moment's hesitation, he was off and running up the beach, the soft bag containing the precious pearl flapping against his thigh.

Chapter 1

'Jemima? Jemima, Wake up!' Max prodded his beloved 11-year-old owner with a velvety grey paw. 'I'm sure it's way past breakfast time, and I'm starving.'

'Hardly!' groaned Jemima, pulling the duvet over her head. 'Go 'way, Max. I'm asleep.'

'No, you're not. You wouldn't be talking to me if you were asleep.' He gave a loud huff, sucking in his cheeks. 'A cat could die of starvation around here, you know.'

Jemima flung the bedcovers away from her face, knowing that resistance was futile. He was never going to let her go back to sleep now. 'Don't exaggerate, Max! As if there's any danger of *you* wasting away!'

'I don't know what you mean,' he answered, an affronted tone creeping into his voice. 'It's just that my stomach's rumbling so loudly that it woke me up. I can't believe you slept through it and...'

She heaved a deep sigh. 'Okay, okay, I give

up – you win!' Jemima swung her legs over the side of the bed and pushed her feet into her slippers. 'Come on, then.'

'Yay,' chirped the large Tonkinese cat, echoing a word he'd picked up from Jemima. He skipped across to the door and followed her downstairs.

'Hey, Jem.' Her twin brother Joe looked up from the comic he was reading at the kitchen table. 'Did you have a good lie-in?'

'Hmm, chance'd be a fine thing,' she grumbled as she forked cat food into Max's bowl.

'Oooh, who got out of bed on the wrong side this morning?' Her brother gave her a lop-sided grin.

'Don't you start,' she replied, pointing the fork at him.

'Blimey, Jem, keep your hair on. It was just a joke.' Joe caught Max's eye, and they both raised their eyebrows, knowing it was best to leave well alone when Jemima was in a grumpy mood. She'd soon snap out of it.

Max buried his muzzle in the bowl, making short work of his meal, before trotting over to the cat flap. After a quick trip out into the garden, he hoped he'd find Jemima back to her usual sunny self upon his return.

'What's wrong, Jem?' asked Joe. 'You okay?'

She sat down with her breakfast cereal, listlessly twirling the spoon around in the bowl. 'I don't know,' she sighed. 'I think it's getting to me, all these trips we've been going on, looking for Mum and Dad. Some of it's been incredibly dangerous, and we've seen so many sad things... but we still haven't found them. I'm starting to worry it's never going to happen, and I guess I'm exhausted too.'

'I know what you mean,' said her brother. 'But just look how far we've come... or should that be how far we've been. Anyway, we must be nearly there – we can't give up now.'

'Yeah, you're right, but it's so hard, isn't it? I must just be having a bad day. Sorry.'

'S'okay,' replied Joe with a wry grin. 'I have plenty of those too, you know, but we just have to keep going. We'll find them, I promise.'

'But *will* we?' she whispered in reply.

'Yeah, we will,' he said with an emphatic nod. 'Cassandra told us so. Don't forget that.'

On their third trip into the past, a Trojan princess with the gift of prophecy had told them of the future reunion with their parents one day. The twins had clung on to that precious nugget of information – it had kept them going all this time and it was vital, because without hope, however tiny a shred it might be, what was the point?

Joe smiled at his sister. 'So, when Charlie comes round this morning, I say we go and see if the old book will let us start on the next chapter. What d'you reckon?'

'Yeah, okay.' Jemima swiped the back of her hand across her eyes, clearing the tears that threatened to spill down her cheeks every time she thought of her missing parents. 'But I must apologise to Max first. I wasn't very nice to him this morning.'

'Don't worry, Jem. He understands.' Joe pushed his floppy fringe off his forehead. 'Blimey, I can't believe I'm saying that about a cat.'

'But he's not just a cat, Joe,' she answered. 'Max could never be *just* a cat.'

Joe snorted. 'No, I guess you're right. And, if there's one thing I wouldn't change about everything that we've been through, it's Max. We'd never have known that he could talk and do all that brave stuff otherwise. I guess we're lucky to have him.'

'Yes, we are.' Jemima swallowed. 'I can't

imagine life without him. He's the most precious thing I have.'

'Oh, cheers,' said her brother. 'Thanks for that. So, you don't think I'm as important as Max, then?'

'Well, if you grow whiskers, a furry coat and a tail, I might reconsider.' Jemima began to giggle.

'Listen, Jem, Charlie will be here soon. I'm going to get dressed.' Joe shot up from the table and headed for the door. 'See you in a bit.'

'Yeah, I'll be ready.' She scooped up the last few spoonfuls of cereal, then took her bowl to the sink to rinse it out. She was feeling better already.

By the time Jemima had showered and dressed, Charlie and Joe were waiting for her to join them in the room where all their journeys into the past started – the room where Uncle Richard kept their parents' things. When she came out of her bedroom, she saw the door was ajar and heard the boys talking in quiet voices. With Max trotting along at her heels, she hurried inside and quietly pushed the door shut behind her.

'Hi, Charlie! You okay?' she asked.

'Hey, Jem,' he replied with a grin. 'Yeah, thanks. We're just talking about the next chapter.'

'Can't wait to see where we end up this time,'

said Joe, as he lifted the antique wooden chest off the shelf. He put it down on the floor and took out the mysterious, old book that was their gateway into the past.

The three children knelt on the rug with the book lying between them. Max huddled beside Jemima, leaning against her as he peered apprehensively at the ancient volume. As always, he could sense it quivering, could see the leather cover twitch as if it might burst open at any moment. He hated the start of these adventures, never knowing where the book would take them and what dangers might await them when they arrived. That first step into the unknown terrified him.

'Ready?' asked Joe.

Charlie nodded, while Jemima reached to unclasp the chain from around her neck.

She laid the necklace with the all-important key on her brother's outstretched palm. 'Here you go.'

They'd done this so many times by now that Joe no longer needed to search for the keyhole. He knew exactly where to find it, cleverly concealed within the intricate golden pattern on the cover. He reckoned he could do it by touch alone, with his eyes closed, if he had to.

As the key turned smoothly in the lock, they all waited to hear the barely audible click. When it came, it was followed by a noise that sounded like the release of a long held-in breath, and the book seemed to expand, freed from its constraints.

'Okey-doke,' said Joe. 'Let's open it.'

Charlie helped him lift the cover and the pages began to flick past at great speed, making a strange whirring sound. Bypassing the first part of the book, they suddenly fell apart with a sharp snap. The next chapter lay open before them, and it had the strangest title.

FISHSTANDINGS

'How ridiculous!' observed Max. 'Everyone knows that fish can't stand – they haven't got legs. That's why they swim instead.'

'Don't forget this is just an anagram, Max,' said Jemima. 'We'll have to change the letters around to reveal the real title.'

'Oh, yes, silly me,' replied the cat, remembering what they'd had to do with every chapter they'd read so far. 'I wonder what it will be this time?'

Jemima placed her forefinger on the F at the

beginning of the word and shifted it to one side. Then, she moved the other letters around until they were all jumbled up.

By now, they were all used to the way that the letters slid across the page with the slightest touch, gliding easily across the surface of the paper but with no danger of falling off. It had seemed so weird the first few times they'd done it, but now they didn't even bother to wonder how it was possible. They just knew it was one of the first pieces of the puzzle that would enable them to unlock the mysteries of the chapter... and ultimately transport them to somewhere in the past.

'So, here we go, guys,' said Jemima. 'Any ideas?'

Charlie scratched his head. 'I can see lots of things, but they're all a bit silly.'

'Like what?' asked Joe.

'Um, *Stands fishing*? *Stash findings*? *Fist hand signs*? That's the best I can do.'

Joe snorted. 'You were right, Charlie. Those sound *really* silly.'

'Well, can you do any better?' asked his sister.

'Maybe. Give me a mo.' Joe stared at the letters. It was hard because they spelled lots of words, but none of them made any sense. 'Okay, what about *Fish and stings*?'

'I don't think that's any better than Charlie's suggestions,' replied Jemima. 'I can see *Fang hiss*... oh, but I can't work out what to do with the letters that are left over.'

'Phew, that's a relief,' said Max, 'because it was starting to sound like something to do with snakes, and I don't want to go anywhere where we're going to meet any of those. You know how I feel about them.'

'All right, Max,' said Charlie. 'No snakes. Let's see what else it might be. Ha, *This finds snags*. That's for sure – it's a great, big *snag*, because we can't solve this one at all.'

'Wait,' said Joe. 'I think I've got it... *Finds Hastings*! We could be going back to 1066 again.'

'But why would we do that?' asked Charlie. 'We've already been there once. We escaped from the Battle of Hastings, so what would be the point of going back again? Besides, we've been moving forward through history with each trip we've been on since then. I don't think we're about to start travelling backwards.'

'*Ssh, infants dig*!' Jemima suddenly exclaimed. 'Perhaps that means it's something to do with archaeology and we've got to dig up treasure or something?'

'Oh yeah, sure,' said her twin brother,

laughing at her suggestion. 'Best take your bucket and spade, then. You might get to make sandcastles while we're there.'

'*Sand*,' repeated Charlie in a quiet voice, his eyes misting over. He took off his glasses and gave them a quick wipe on the hem of his t-shirt, something he always did when he was thinking.

Jemima and Joe stared at him, waiting patiently. They knew better than to interrupt their super-brainy friend when the thinking process was going on – they could almost hear the cogs turning in his mind.

'Yes, *sand*,' he repeated, blinking as he gazed into the distance at some invisible object only he could see. 'Hmm, yes... that's it. I think I've got it.'

'What is it, then?' asked Jemima, fizzing with impatience. 'Come on, Charlie. Tell us!'

He took a deep breath, prolonging the moment and pushing the twins' patience to its limits.

'Charlie!' cried Joe. 'Spit it out, for goodness sake.'

'Shifting sands,' breathed Charlie.

'Shifting sands?' repeated Joe, with a frown. 'What's that supposed to mean? If that's it, I don't see where the book will be sending us.'

Jemima agreed with him, apart from one

thing – when she heard Charlie say the two words, she'd felt a shiver of recognition, as if something was telling her that he was right.

'I guess the only way to be sure is by trying it,' she said and began to shift the letters to spell out the two words. Her fingers tingled as she moved each one, a clear sign that something unusual was happening... and, sure enough, as she slid the final S into position, the title *Shifting Sands* lit up, each letter glowing brightly against the page.

'So, it's right,' said Charlie with a frown. 'That *is* the title.'

'But I still don't get it,' said Joe. 'Shifting Sands? What does that mean? Where's it going to take us?'

'Not sure,' said Charlie. 'I can't think of any famous historical event about sand.'

'Hey, perhaps the poem will help us to work it out?' said Jemima.

A short rhyme was printed on the lower half of the page beneath the title, just as in every other chapter so far. These little verses always provided extra clues if the anagram was too hard to decipher.

'Okay then,' began Jemima, 'let's see if this

helps.' She started to recite the lines out loud,

'Your journey starts in desert lands,

To find Atlantis of the Sands.

Deep underground the treasure lies,

Long hidden from all searching eyes.'

She sat back on her heels. 'Hmm, well I don't think that's any use at all. Atlantis of the Sands? Where on earth's that?'

'Don't know,' replied Joe. 'But I like the sound of finding treasure. D'you think there'll be pirates?'

Jemima turned to Charlie. 'What do you think? Have you heard of it?'

He shook his head. 'Nope. We need to do some research. I could go and fetch my iPad from next door.'

'Or we could ask Uncle Richard?' said Jemima. 'I bet he'd know.'

'No way,' answered her brother. 'He'd ask why we want to know and where we'd heard about it, then he'd go all weird like he usually does when we talk about stuff like that with him.'

Jemima glanced at Max, and it was at that moment she realised he'd gone very quiet. The cat's eyes were wide and staring, and she could only describe the look she could see reflected in his turquoise gaze as one of complete shock.

'Max, what is it?' she asked gently. 'Whatever's the matter?'

'I think *I* know,' he whispered.

'Know what?' asked Joe.

'The answer,' murmured Max. He looked afraid now. 'I think *I* know where Atlantis of the Sands is.'

'*You*? Don't be silly,' snorted Joe. 'How would *you* know?'

Max turned to look at him. 'Because I've been there – that's how.'

'Yeah, in your dreams,' replied Joe with a laugh. 'You're just spouting rubbish, as usual. Seriously, Max, I'm starting to wonder if you're losing your marbles.'

'*Losing my marbles*?' spluttered the cat. 'How dare you?'

Joe rolled his eyes. 'Hey, keep your fur on, Max! I was just saying...'

'Shut up, Joe,' snapped Jemima. 'And let him speak.'

Chapter 2

Guardians of Time Headquarters

Meanwhile, in a secret location, far, far away, a mysterious gathering of shadowy figures sat around a large table, discussing that day's agenda.

'I'm sorry, but why are we sending the young time-travellers to this place?' said one of the more junior members of the group. 'It doesn't sound like a historical life-or-death situation – not like some of the other more pressing matters we have on our list.'

'I'm glad you asked that question, Octavius,' replied the Master. 'I'm sure that many of you are also thinking the same thing, so please allow me to explain.'

All eyes turned towards him as the Master glanced around the table to make sure everyone was paying attention.

'As Octavius has rightly pointed out,' he began, 'this might seem an unusual mission to send our agents on but it's something that was started when the cat was taken to Arabia against his will.

Most of you here know what happened on that occasion.'

The assembled guardians nodded in response, remembering Max's solo Arabian adventure.

'Good. Well, as you no doubt recall, none of it was of our doing,' continued the Master. 'Instead, a shady character named Salazar infiltrated the *Shadows of the Past* book by foul means and snatched 009 Lives to do his evil bidding. The magician has since been dealt with and will cause no further trouble, but I've decided that the cat must finish what he started... before our young Chrononauts can continue with their next mission.'

The Master turned to the young guardian who'd spoken up, bestowing a benevolent smile upon him. 'But, Octavius, there is something I must point out. Although this wasn't part of our original plans for them and, however strange it might appear, this journey *will* have a significant historical impact.'

'Will they *all* be accompanying the cat on this trip?' asked his second-in-command. '009 Lives went there on his own last time.'

'It wouldn't be fair to send him alone again,' said the Master. 'Besides, four heads are better than one. So, let's see what happens where ancient magic stirs beneath the sand and fate begins to reveal its hand.' Steepling his fingers together, he gave an enigmatic smile.

As he spoke, a large screen on the wall behind him flickered into life, and the Guardians of Time sat back in their seats, making themselves comfortable as they prepared to watch the adventure unfold.

'Let the action begin,' said the Master, raising his right hand...

Chapter 3

Max had already told Jemima about his Arabian adventure, once he'd recovered from the shock of his ordeal. To be honest, Jemima thought he'd probably dreamt the whole thing. It sounded rather too much like the tale of Aladdin that Dad used to read to the twins at bedtime. Max had always been snuggled up beside her, so he'd have listened too and would have been familiar with the story. She still wasn't convinced any of it had really happened but decided to let him have his say.

'Go on then, Max,' she said. 'Tell us what you know.'

'Well, it was the bit about the "treasure underground" in the rhyme that made me think it's the same place,' he said, an earnest expression on his handsome face. 'That and the desert sands.'

'The same place as what, Max?' asked Joe, his lip curling in disbelief. 'When did you ever go somewhere like that?'

'Remember what happened the last time we

travelled back into the past, Joe?' snapped his sister. 'When we met King Charles II, it turned out that Max already knew him because he'd been on a solo adventure into the past without us. And he also went to Mistley Thorn on his own before we went back there with him to defeat the Witchfinder. Oh, and let's not forget his trip with Father Christmas.'

'Okay, okay, I get it,' Joe replied reluctantly. 'But you should have told Charlie and me. We're all in this together, so you shouldn't be keeping secrets from us.'

Jemima didn't want to admit in front of Max that she hadn't actually believed the tale of his escapade in the Arabian desert at the time. 'I just didn't think it was relevant,' she said. 'How was I to know that this was going to happen?'

Joe and Charlie shared a glance that seemed to imply they weren't too impressed before turning towards Jemima with an accusing stare.

Even Max gave her a sideways look, not sure that he liked her description of what had been a harrowing experience for him as not "relevant".

Knowing they were probably right, Jemima wriggled uncomfortably. 'Well, anyway, let's hear what he's got to say,' she said quickly. 'Fire away,

Max. We're all ears.'

Max didn't really know where to begin. 'Um, well, it all started when I was in this room and the old book was open on the floor. I did think that was a bit strange because Joe always puts it away in the wooden box when we come back from one of our trips into the past.'

'I do,' said Joe. 'So how did it end up on the floor?'

'I don't know,' replied the cat. 'But I heard a voice asking me to come closer and to turn a page with my paw. I wish I hadn't gone anywhere near it now, but I did and, the next moment a hand shot out between the pages and grabbed my leg. Then, it pulled me inside the book. There was a flash and a bang and, whoosh, I was gone. I hadn't a clue where I was. All I knew was that it was hot and dusty, and I was scared – really scared.'

Remembering what had happened suddenly brought it all rushing back and Max had to gulp back a lump that rose in his throat, preventing him from speaking. Then, he started to gabble, with hardly a pause for breath, trying to get it all out.

'So, it was in this old town in the middle of nowhere, and I was at the house of this horrible man – an evil magician. He said he'd brought me there to do a job for him. The next day, he put me in a bag attached to his donkey's saddle, and we travelled through the desert for hours until we got there. Then he shoved me down through a trapdoor and told me to fetch a lamp, but when I brought it back he tried to trick me. So, I wouldn't give it to him and he left me down there, all alone in the dark, and he rode off. I thought I'd never get out and that I'd die down there, trapped underground.' The large cat's chest heaved as he recalled his panic at that moment.

'Slow down, Max,' said Jemima in a soothing voice. 'Take your time. Tell the boys what you told me.'

'Yeah,' said Joe. 'Because, so far, this isn't making much sense. Why did this magician chap want you to fetch a lamp, and what was it doing underground in the middle of the desert?'

Max took a deep breath. 'It was a magic lamp, I think.'

'Like in the story of Aladdin,' added Jemima, interrupting him.

''Yes, and it was in a tunnel,' he continued. 'The magician had to find a trapdoor and then he lowered me down in a basket. Inside, there was a passageway with doors, and different chambers filled with treasure – gold, silver, and jewels.'

Joe's eyes opened wide at the mention of treasure. 'Blimey! Why didn't this guy ask you to bring him some of that instead? What did he want with a stupid old lamp?'

'That's what I wondered too,' said Max. 'He told me not to go into the rooms where the treasure was but to find a garden with a tree.'

'Oh, come off it, Max, this isn't real,' scoffed Joe. 'A garden? A tree can't grow underground – trees need light and water. You *must* have been dreaming.'

'No,' shouted Max, beginning to get cross. 'Stop interrupting me. I'm telling the truth. Do you want to hear this or not?'

'We *do*, Max,' replied Charlie. 'Tell us your story.'

'Yes, and you can be quiet, Joe,' said Jemima. 'Let him finish. Carry on, Max.'

Max gave a loud sniff. 'I will, but only if certain people stop telling me I imagined it.'

'All right, I've got the message,' said Joe. He mimed pulling a zipper across his mouth. 'I won't say another word.'

'Hmm, I'll believe that when I see it,' harrumphed the cat. 'Now, where was I? Ah yes...

so I found the garden and in the middle stood a big tree. It was covered in flowers that smelled beautiful.' Max stopped, hearing a sharp intake of breath from Joe as if he was about to say something.

Noticing the cat glare at him, Joe quickly snapped his mouth shut and gestured with his hand for Max to continue.

'The lamp was hidden high up in the branches, but I managed to shake it down,' said Max. 'Then I took it back to where the trapdoor was. The man lowered the basket and told me to put the lamp in it, but I didn't trust him. Something told me that he'd take the lamp and leave me down there. So, I told him I wouldn't do it and that I'd bring the lamp up with me. He made all kinds of excuses why that wasn't possible, but I stood my ground. You'll never guess what he did next?'

'Did he come down there himself?' asked Charlie. 'In fact, I don't get why he didn't just come down and fetch the lamp in the first place.'

'It was something to do with magic,' said Max. 'Because I had to give certain information before the doors would open in the tunnel. It had to be me, for some reason, which I still don't get either. But you're wrong, Charlie – he didn't climb down and get the lamp off me. He started shouting curses and then he slammed the trapdoor shut, leaving me trapped down there in the dark. Then I heard the donkey's hoofbeats disappearing into the distance.' The cat's eyes welled with tears as he remembered his terror when that happened.

'OMG, Max,' said Charlie. 'You poor thing. That must have been horrible.'

Even Joe felt sorry for Max when he heard this and reached out to give the cat a comforting pat. 'How did you get out?' he asked.

'I went back to where the garden was and sat under the tree. I really thought my life was going to end there, but then I saw a small creature scurry past and realised it must have got in somehow, so I followed it. When I smelt fresh air, I knew there had to be a way out and eventually I crawled through a gap between some rocks.'

'Phew,' said Charlie. 'But what happened next?'

Max sighed. 'I didn't realise at that point that my troubles were only just beginning.'

'What d'you mean?' asked Joe, now intrigued by the cat's story.

'Well, it was cool underground,' said Max. 'But once I was outside it started to get hotter and hotter… and hotter. The sun was burning me like you wouldn't believe. There was no shade and I had nothing to drink. All I could see was miles and miles of sand dunes in every direction. I tried to keep going, but I think I collapsed and I almost died.'

Jemima had already heard Max's story, but she hadn't believed it was real. Now, listening to him describe his ordeal again, she realised how much he must have suffered… and just how close she'd come to losing him.

'Oh, Max,' she whispered, her eyes filling with tears. 'I'm so sorry, I'm so sorry.'

'I didn't think I'd see any of you ever again,' he croaked, sniffling back a sob.

'But you're still here, Max,' said Charlie. 'You came back. How did that happen?'

The cat took a moment to control his emotions before replying. 'I was lucky, very lucky. You see, two kindly souls found me and they saved my life. I wouldn't be here now if they hadn't helped me.'

'Who were they?' asked Joe. 'And what were they doing out there in the middle of a desert?'

'Falak was the one who first spotted me,' explained Max. 'He was a falcon. In fact, I'm ashamed to say that I thought he was going to eat me. But, instead, he fetched his friend Ghazala and they carried me to an oasis.'

'Blimey,' said Joe. 'They must have been strong... to carry *you*, I mean. Did they fly with you in their talons?'

'No, don't be silly,' snapped Max. 'Ghazala wasn't a falcon. She was a camel and she carried me on her back. So, they put me in the shade to rest and fetched me food and water. We stayed there until I recovered.'

'But you were still in the desert,' said Charlie. 'How were you able to come home?'

'It was a miracle,' answered Max. Even now, thinking back, he still couldn't quite believe it himself. 'I knew I probably had to go back to the place where I first arrived, because that's what you say we have to do every time we travel back into the past. So, Falak and Ghazala worked out where the town probably was and they took me there. Then they had to leave before anyone saw them. I found the magician's house and was going to ask him to send me home, seeing as he was the one who'd brought me there.'

The large cat gave a deep sigh and shook his head.

'Did he refuse?' asked Joe.

'Worse than that,' said Max. 'He wasn't there. The house was locked, bolted and barred. A stray cat in the street outside told me that the magician had disappeared.'

'This story goes from bad to worse, Max,' said Charlie. 'Why didn't you tell us any of this before?'

'I did tell someone. I told Jemima,' said Max, shooting her another sideways look. 'But, to be honest, it was such a terrifying experience that I just wanted to forget all about it.'

'So, if the magician was nowhere to be found, how did you make it back here?' asked Joe. 'I don't get it.'

'Well, you might find *this* hard to believe too,' said Max. 'But it was all thanks to the jeans chap with no legs.'

Jemima knew what he was referring to – and this was a major part of his tale that she'd struggled to believe before – but the two boys were completely flummoxed by this.

'How could he be wearing jeans if he had no legs?' asked Joe with a puzzled frown.

'He means a *genie*,' explained Jemima. 'The genie in the lamp.'

'Oh, come off it, Max,' said Joe. 'A genie? You mean like in Aladdin? They're not real. Now I know for sure you're making this up. Have you been pulling our leg all along?'

'Pulling your leg? How dare you? How else do you think I got back here? On a magic carpet, perhaps?'

'Well, that would make as much sense,' snorted Joe.

Max growled. 'I wonder why I waste my breath sometimes. You clearly haven't listened to a word I've said. Why doesn't anyone believe me?'

'Calm down, Max,' murmured Jemima, gently stroking his head. 'We *do* believe you, but it's a very strange story, that's all. It's a bit difficult to get our heads around all this. So, tell the boys about the genie.'

'The genie that was *real*, you mean?'

Jemima nodded. 'Yes, *that* one. Go on.'

The cat sniffed, glaring at Joe as he continued with his tale. 'Well, I'd given up all hope by that point and I started to cry. One of my tears landed on the lamp and I wiped it off with my paw, Suddenly, there was a loud bang and this monster appeared before me.'

'The genie,' said Jemima.

'Yes, *him*,' answered Max. 'He called me "Master" and asked what my wish was. In fact, what he actually said was "*As-sam wa t'taa ah*". I didn't know what he meant by "my wish" and said that I just wanted to go home. Then, he said "*Ma'a salaama*! Go in peace." I saw a flash of bright light and my head began to spin. The next thing I knew was that I was back here.'

Max had just recited two phrases in Arabic, perhaps without even realising it. Thanks to the magic golden owl charm attached to his collar, the same as the ones Jemima, Joe and Charlie wore on chains around their necks, they were all instantly able to understand any foreign language they heard, be it ancient or modern, human or animal. But this was what finally convinced the three children that the cat had been telling the truth after all.

'I'm sorry, Max,' said Joe, looking contrite. 'It all sounded just like something from a fairy tale, but I really do believe you now.'

Max nodded, despite still feeling a bit cross with him. 'Okay, apology accepted,' he said.

'So, we're going to the same place you went to, Max,' said Jemima. 'But where exactly in the world *is* Atlantis of the Sands?'

'I'm not sure,' replied the large cat. 'But Falak and Ghazala told me I was in Arabia and they mentioned the name of the desert, but I can't remember it now. Ah, hang on, they did say it was known as... er, the Empty Quarter, I think.'

'Arabia makes sense,' said Charlie. 'The story of the Magic Lamp is from the tales of *The Arabian Nights*. But I've never heard of the Empty Quarter.'

'Well, what are we waiting for?' asked Joe, as impatient as ever to set off on another adventure into the unknown.

'So, we're going to a place that we think is somewhere in Arabia and our clue is the Shifting Sands,' said Jemima. 'And it's something to do with treasure and a lost city called Atlantis of the Sands – but that's all we know.'

'Yes,' said Charlie, looking over his shoulder. 'And look, the portal is already here.'

They all turned around to see a strange cloud of mist hovering just above the floor behind them. They'd done this many times by now and knew this was their gateway into the past. All they had to do was step inside its murky depths and they'd be transported back in time. A warm breeze swirled around them, ruffling their hair, and the hot, dusty scent of faraway lands filled their nostrils.

'So, do we go right *now*?' asked Jemima.

'Of course,' replied her brother. 'No point in waiting, is there? Come on. Let's do it.'

She started to protest. 'But maybe we should...?'

Joe didn't wait to hear what she was going to say. He grabbed her wrist, pulling her to her feet.

'No, wait. I've got to make sure I've got hold of Max,' said Jemima. Losing him would be her worst nightmare and was the thing she dreaded most on these journeys. She wrapped the cat tightly in her arms as the two boys linked hands, forming a circle with Jemima in the middle.

Together, they shuffled sideways into the mist, moving further into its clammy embrace until, with a loud whoosh, everything went black.

They'd vanished. Its job done, the misty cloud began to thin, until even the last remaining wispy tendrils had disappeared, leaving no trace that it had ever been there at all.

Chapter 4

Round and round they whirled, the wind roaring in their ears as they tumbled headfirst through the twisting passageways of time. It never got any easier – if anything, it seemed to get worse each time they did it. It felt as if unseen forces were trying to tear them apart, but they clung to one another as if their lives depended on it. If any of them got separated, who knew where they might end up?

Just when it felt as if they could take no more, they passed through a blinding flash of light and were expelled from the time vortex with a violent thrust that sent them sprawling on the ground.

'Ugh,' cried Joe. 'Paah, paah.' He'd landed face down and his mouth was full of sand, which he was now trying to spit out. 'Yuck, yuck, yuck!'

'Hey, you okay?' asked Charlie who was lying beside him. Luckily, he'd ended up on his back.

'Oh, yeah, apart from feeling like I've swallowed a whopping great sandcastle.' Joe ground the grains of sand between his teeth – it wasn't a pleasant sensation. He was now on all fours, still spitting out mouthfuls of gritty saliva.

Jemima sat up, relieved to find Max still encircled in her arms. His eyelids remained tightly closed. 'It's safe to open your eyes now,' she whispered in his ear. 'We've arrived.'

Hearing the gentle swish of waves lapping against the shore, she turned around. 'Ooh, this is lovely!' The crystal turquoise waters of the Arabian Gulf sparkled in the early morning sun, but the white sand was almost too bright to look at and she had to shield her eyes with her hand.

'Um, I'm a little worried,' said Max.

'Worried? Why?' Jemima asked.

The cat cast a quick look around. 'Well, this wasn't what I was expecting. It looks nothing like the last time I was here. There wasn't any sea and no beach – just miles and miles of sand dunes. I don't think we're in the right place. Or maybe I got it wrong, and this *Shifting Sands* thing is nothing to do with the time I came to Arabia on my own.'

Joe jumped to his feet. 'Oh, great! Thanks, Max. We should have known better than to listen to you and your tales of magic lamps. *Now* what are we supposed to do?'

'This isn't my fault,' said the cat. 'How was I to know?'

'That's about right.' Joe curled his lip. 'You know nothing, and I can't believe we let you blather on about all that...'

'Stop it, Joe,' said Jemima, interrupting him. 'We were coming here anyway, because it's where the book was going to send us. It makes no difference whether it's the same place as the one Max knows, or not.'

Joe scowled. 'Yeah, yeah, stand up for your precious Max. You always take his side.'

'Hey,' Charlie yelled suddenly. 'Let's stop this.' Standing between the twins, he made a calming gesture with his hands. 'Arguing about it doesn't solve anything, Joe. Jemima's right – we're here because the book has sent us to this place. And don't take it out on Max. He's not to blame.'

This was quite a speech for Charlie, and the twins gazed back at him in surprise, both lost for words after his outburst. Max simply responded with a grateful smile.

'So, what do we do now?' asked Jemima. 'We have no idea where we are.'

'Well, wherever it is, it's flippin' hot,' said Charlie. 'I'm going for a paddle.' He kicked off his trainers, feeling the soft, white sand ooze between his toes as he ran down the beach and into the warm, shallow water. Almost blinded by the dazzling sunlight, Charlie blinked as he gazed out across the waves. It was an idyllic scene – so peaceful, not a single boat out there, not another person in sight – nothing, apart from the rhythmic hush of the waves and the calls of seabirds overhead.

He looked from left to right... and that's when he saw him, right at the far end of the shore. A boy, maybe eleven or twelve, crouched near the edge of the water. His tunic was soaked and torn, and he clutched a small woven bag in one hand. The boy's black hair stuck to his face and, when he turned, Charlie could see the fear in his dark eyes.

'Hey,' Charlie called out, raising a hand. 'Are you okay?'

The boy flinched and stood up fast, backing away as if he was in danger.

'I'm not... I mean, I won't hurt you,' Charlie said in a calm voice. 'I'm with my friends.' He waved his hand, gesturing to where Jemima and Joe sat, further back up the beach. 'We, um, we're a bit lost – we don't know where we are.'

The boy frowned. He understood Charlie perfectly but had no idea that it was because of the magic golden owl charm that Charlie was wearing.

Charlie called to the twins. 'Hey, you two, come down here.'

Surprised to see Charlie with a stranger, the twins stood up and hurried to join him.

Charlie tried again. 'We don't mean you any harm,' he said.

The boy hesitated, then nodded.

'Great. Okay. I'm Charlie, and these are my friends, Joe and Jemima. What's your name?'

The boy shot a nervous look back up the beach, then whispered, 'Zayed.'

'What's wrong, Zayed?' asked Charlie. 'You look like you're in trouble.'

Zayed's mouth tightened. He glanced behind him again, then finally said, 'Pirates. They took my father. I escaped.'

Joe's ears pricked up at this. 'Pirates? Like... *real* ones?' he asked, his eyes glinting with excitement.

Zayed gave him a look that said, *what else would I mean?*

'But why did they take your father?' asked Jemima, horrified by what he'd told them.

'We dive for pearls,' replied Zayed. 'That's what we do in the summer months. But these men... I think they came for more than pearls. They know my father is the leader of our tribe. They want to ransom him.'

Charlie's head was spinning. *Pearls? Pirates? Tribes?* 'But where is your tribe, Zayed?'

'A long way from here. In the Rub' al Khali desert – the Empty Quarter.'

Charlie, Joe and Jemima's eyes opened wide when he mentioned this. It was a name they recognised, and a quick glance passed between the three of them.

'Um, how long would it take to get there?' asked Jemima.

'Many days, probably, but I'm not entirely sure of the way, so I hope I don't get lost. I can't go back to the port where we keep our fishing boat, because they'll probably search there first.' Zayed's eyes scanned the beach. 'I think they might already be hunting for me.'

Charlie's stomach tightened. 'So, what shall we do?'

'I think I need to go back to the desert, to find my people,' said Zayed. 'You said "*we*". Do you mean you'll come with me?'

Charlie glanced at the twins, then nodded. 'Er, I... I guess so. We're not leaving you alone, So, yeah, we'll come.'

Zayed blinked in surprise. 'Really? We've only just met. You're strange, Charlie. But good.'

Charlie grinned. 'That's what my mum says.'

Zayed turned to the twins. 'Are you sure you're both okay with this? Coming with me?"

'Of course,' replied Jemima. 'Like Charlie said, we're not going to leave you on your own.' She didn't mention they had an ulterior motive for wanting to accompany him to the Empty Quarter. 'And there's someone else who'll be coming with us too – someone we haven't introduced you to yet.'

As the boy's eyes darted nervously around the beach, wondering who else was there, Jemima ran to pick up Max.

'Zayed, meet Max, my cat. Wherever we go, he goes too. I hope you don't mind.'

The relief on the boy's face was clear and he gave a broad grin. 'Far from it. I love cats. Pleased to meet you, Max.' He was startled to see the cat dip its head in greeting as it held out a paw to him.

'Right, well, let's go, shall we?' Joe said quickly, before Max spoke and frightened Zayed off before they'd even left the beach.

They moved quickly, up over the dunes and away from the sea. Zayed was sure-footed, as if he knew every grain of sand he stepped on. Charlie stumbled a few times, not used to walking in this heat, but Zayed helped him back up. They kept going until they came upon a few palm trees beside a small pool of precious water.

During the hottest part of the day, they rested there in the shade. Zayed scooted up one of the tree trunks and picked handfuls of fresh dates, which he threw down for them to eat. Once it began to cool down a little they set off again, rested and refreshed.

As the sun dipped lower, painting the sky in hues of gold and crimson, they reached a narrow valley carved into the land by time and the wind.

'We should try to sleep here,' said Zayed, already gathering handfuls of dry vegetation for a tiny fire. 'But let's stay alert, in case the pirates are already following us.'

Charlie and the twins agreed. This was Zayed's world and he knew best. With any luck, their new friend would lead them to the place they needed to find. They looked up at the bright stars beginning to prick the ink-black sky and shivered, partly from the sudden drop in temperature, but also at the thought that the pirates might be on their trail.

In the last shreds of twilight, the four children chatted, trying to chase away their fears before total darkness fell.

'What exactly happened when the pirates took your father?' asked Jemima.

Zayed told them about the last few moments on the dhow before the pirates came aboard. He still didn't mention the pearl – he didn't know these strangers well enough yet. They would have to earn his trust. But he remembered his father's last words to him before Zayed had jumped over the side and escaped. "Keep the pearl safe, my son... at all costs." Zayed prayed that those *costs* hadn't included his father's life.

Instead, he warned the children of the possible dangers that lay ahead. Not only must his new friends watch out for the pirates catching up with them, but they must also be on their guard for sandstorms, scorpions, and snakes.

All of these were terrifying enough to make Jemima think she'd never get to sleep. But, no sooner had darkness fallen than they were cocooned in a blanket of silence, and she'd dropped off before she knew it, with Max snuggled up in her arms for warmth. The cat wished he could talk to her as usual but hadn't dared utter a word yet, with Zayed there.

Chapter 5

They awoke to the sound of sand hissing across the dry, barren ground. The sky was barely blue, with dawn only just beginning to stretch her long, rosy fingers across the desert. Zayed was already awake, crouched by the last embers of the small fire, poking at the ashes.

'We must go,' he said. 'Before the wind rises.'

The children nodded, rubbing sleep from their eyes.

'Where are we heading?' asked Joe.

'I think there's a well two hills from here,' replied Zayed. 'After that, open desert.'

They set out as the sun began to climb in the sky, the dunes glowing gold and copper underfoot.

As they clambered to the crest of the second hill, Jemima turned to Zayed, her throat parched. 'Is it much further to the well?' she croaked, barely able to speak. And she was worried about Max. He desperately needed a drink too.

'Almost there,' Zayed answered, pointing at the flat land stretching out below them.

'I can't believe we were stupid enough to come here unprepared for this – no water bottles, hats, sunglasses or sun cream,' said Jemima. 'I mean, we knew we were coming to the desert and that it would be hot. What were we thinking? If only *someone* hadn't made us leave in such a rush...' She looked pointedly at her brother.

Zayed gave her a strange look. He had no idea what Jemima was talking about. Sunglasses? Sun cream? But he agreed with her about lacking what they needed for crossing the desert – food, water, clothes to protect them from the sun... and camels.

'We must take great care,' he said. 'The desert can be a killer.'

'Oh, great, one more thing to worry about,' thought Jemima as they began their descent.

When they reached the foot of the hill, they didn't see the well at first – just three twisted old palm trees, some animal bones and a scattering of faded pottery shards which lay half-buried in the sand.

At that precise moment, the sun rose a little higher in the sky, causing a shaft of light to reflect off a piece of broken pottery embedded in the ground. It illuminated a round shape in the sand.

'There it is,' exclaimed Zayed. 'Help me uncover it.'

Working together, the children swept away the sand with their bare hands, revealing the stone lip of a well with strange symbols etched upon it – tribal markings mixed with star patterns. Protected by a rocky outcrop overhead, the well was covered by a circular slab of desert stone. When the boys moved it aside, they found a sunken basin with steps leading down in a spiral.

'This is a bit weird,' said Joe. 'What's a well doing out here in the middle of nowhere?'

'It was built many years ago for the caravans who cross this route,' Zayed explained.

Joe's eyebrows flew up. '*Caravans*? Out here in the desert?' Joe's idea of caravans was rather different to the ones Zayed was familiar with, and he imagined long queues of them, with their wheels stuck in the sand. In Arabia, however, caravans were groups of people, mostly traders, travelling great distances across desert areas. They often carried luxury goods, such as silks, perfumes, spices, and jewellery, so journeying together gave them protection from bandits.

Zayed traced his finger over the carved symbols. 'This is just one of many ancient stopping points for travellers. They were hidden to prevent our enemies from stealing or even poisoning the water. Some of them are lost now, buried by sandstorms or just collapsed. Let's hope this one still has some water for us.' He dropped a piece of broken pottery down the well and they all heard an unmistakable splash as it fell to the bottom.

'Yay,' cried Jemima, who'd been crossing her fingers so hard that they hurt.

Zayed began to climb carefully down the steps, with Joe following close behind. Charlie and Jemima remained at the top with Max, who'd been alarmingly quiet for a while now.

They heard Joe's voice from below. 'There's water down here but no rope or bucket, so we can't bring any up to the surface.'

'What are we going to do?' asked Jemima.

'We'll all just have to come down here to drink,' Joe called up to the top. 'It's the only way.'

'Wait,' cried Charlie. 'I've found something.' He'd been probing the soft sand around the well with his fingers and suddenly touched a hard object beneath the surface. Like a dog looking for a buried bone, he began to dig furiously, sending sand flying in all directions.

'Hey, watch what you're doing, Charlie,' Jemima grumbled.

'But look what I've found,' he crowed, holding his prize aloft. Grasping the clay pot in his hand, he leant over the edge of the well. 'Here you are, Joe. This might help.'

Joe climbed back up and took it from him. 'Great! Well done, mate!'

It took several trips up and down the stone spiral steps to fetch enough water for them all to drink their fill – Max included.

The water from the well was surprisingly clear and cool, despite the heat. Fed by an underground spring that filtered through layers of mineral-rich stone, it tasted sweet and pure and, to the thirsty travellers, it seemed like the most wonderful thing they'd ever drunk.

As they sat under the shade of the overhanging rock to recover, Zayed climbed one of the palm trees and brought down a supply of fresh dates to take with them. While they rested, they tried to work out which way they should go, seeing the vastness of the desert spread out before them.

'The sensible thing would be to stay here until the sun starts to go down,' said Zayed. 'We should switch to desert travel rhythm.'

'What's that?' asked Joe.

'We walk at night and in the early morning while it's cool,' Zayed explained. 'Then we rest during the hottest part of the day.'

So, they stayed by the well, snoozing in the shade of the palm trees and the rocky outcrop above their heads.

While the others dozed, Max trotted a small distance away and quickly dug a hole. This was the biggest litter tray he'd ever seen! As he covered over his business, he noticed some marks in the sand. If he wasn't mistaken, they looked like camel tracks and they were leading away from the well. The footprints were partially buried but looked fresh enough to follow. He hurried back to tell Jemima, whispering quietly in her ear.

When Zayed awoke, Jemima showed him the tracks.

'Yes, camels,' he said. 'Most likely from a recent caravan. They might not be far away. Well spotted, Jemima!'

She winked at Max. She'd couldn't tell Zayed that it was actually the cat who'd found them but felt guilty for taking the credit, nonetheless.

The sun eventually began to sink down

towards the horizon and the air grew cool around them. As evening fell, the sky transformed into a magical backcloth of deep-blue velvet, studded with a million twinkling stars. They lay on their backs, gazing up at the wondrous sight.

'There's no light pollution,' said Charlie. 'We never see anything like this at home.'

Zayed didn't understand what Charlie meant by "light pollution", but he quickly seized on the word "home". 'So where exactly are you from?' he asked. He'd been wondering about this since they'd first met, but none of them had spoken of it.

Charlie shot a glance at the twins. Did they dare to risk telling him the truth? Jemima shook her head. No, at least not yet. 'Er, we're from another country far from here,' said Charlie.

Zayed grinned. 'Well, I'd worked that much out, looking the way you do. What's it called? Your country, I mean?'

'England,' Charlie replied.

Baffled by the name, Zayed shook his head. 'Never heard of it.'

'I'm not surprised,' said Charlie. 'It really is a very long way away.'

Zayed raised his eyebrows. 'So why have you come here?'

Charlie pursed his lips. 'You know what? We're not entirely sure, but I think we're here to find out.'

That hadn't exactly answered Zayed's question, but it happened to be true, and they all burst out laughing.

They drank more of the delicious water which Joe went down into the well to fetch, and they nibbled on some of the fresh dates – which tasted nothing like the wrinkly, dried ones the children had tried at home. Even Max had to eat some of the fruit, because there was nothing else for him, which Jemima felt bad about. He was always pestering her to bring some of his cat food on their trips into the past. She should have listened and resolved to remember next time.

'These carvings around the well – the symbols and star patterns – aren't just decoration, you know,' said Zayed, tracing his finger over them. 'I recognise some of them. They're my tribe's markings.'

Charlie stared intently at the carvings. 'So they must mean something,' he said. Intrigued, he looked closer and suddenly noticed that one set of symbols lined up with the current position of the moon and stars above their heads. 'Hey, I think I know what this might be.'

Charlie gazed up at the sky once more. 'It's a kind of map of the heavens – a celestial compass. Look!' They all followed his finger as he pointed at the symbols and then up at the stars. 'Do you see what I mean?'

'It's showing us the way,' said Zayed. 'The constellations carved in the stone match the night sky and indicate the route we must follow. Well done, Charlie.' He shot his new friend an admiring glance. 'Right, I think we should get moving. Are you all ready?'

They stood up, dusting the sand off their clothes, almost shivering now as the night-time air grew chilly. Walking would warm them up.

As they set out from the well, looking up at the sky as they followed the clues in the carvings, a sudden breeze rose up, swirling around them in the darkness. The wind seemed to speak in whispers, low voices curling through the air like secrets.

At first, they thought it was just the sound of the wind playing tricks, but then they all heard the same thing – a voice calling Zayed's name... in his own language, a dialect that the 21st-century time-travelling youngsters shouldn't have known, if it hadn't been for their magic owl charms.

'Beware! You are being followed,' it warned. 'They are not far behind.'

Jemima's blood ran cold. 'Where's that coming from? Who is it?'

'I don't know,' said Zayed. 'It could be a desert spirit or a Djinn?' He was putting on a brave face, but the tremor in his voice betrayed his fear. Djinns were sometimes bad.

'Did it mean the pirates?' whispered Charlie. 'They're not far behind?'

'Maybe,' said Zayed, casting an uneasy glance over his shoulder. '*Yalla* – Let's keep going.'

The voice stayed with them, a constant background whisper as they hurried through the desert, desperate to put as much distance as possible between themselves and whoever was coming after them.

That night, the sand around them glowed faintly under the moonlight – tiny glints, like eyes watching from the dunes.

Daylight came at last, bringing with it a welcome sense of relief after the terrors of the night. But it wasn't long before heat and exhaustion began to play tricks on them.

As Joe squinted into the distance, he suddenly cried out, pointing to where he'd spotted palm trees in the shimmer of the heat haze. ‘Hey, is that an oasis?’ He started to move towards it, drawn by its magical allure.

‘Wait,’ said Zayed. Something about the sight of it had spooked him and, despite the heat, a shiver ran down his spine. Perhaps this was the place he’d heard of in some of the tribal stories recounted around the campfire? Known as *The Oasis of the Forgotten*, it was a place that lured lost travellers with the promise of water and shade, but none ever returned from it. But, in spite of his misgivings, he followed the others as they hurried towards it.

Desperate for water, they approached the oasis. When they reached it, everything appeared perfect... too perfect. The surface of the water was completely still, like a mirror, reflecting the intense blue of the sky above. The trees didn’t move at all – not even a hint of a rustle amongst the palm fronds.

Joe reached out to touch the water and saw his reflection blink... but it blinked a moment before *he* did. What? He tried again and the same thing happened. How was that possible?

At a frantic signal from Zayed, they all backed slowly away. As they turned to look back at the oasis, the illusion rippled and disappeared. All that remained was an empty patch of sand. They'd had a lucky escape.

Chapter 6

As the sun climbed higher in the sky and the temperature rose, the sand shimmered, and a dark shape moved on the horizon.

'Wait,' Zayed whispered, pulling Charlie down behind a rise in a dune. 'Look over there! Do you see it?'

At first Charlie thought it was a trick of the heat – just a mirage – but then the shape came into focus. It was a camel, tall and elegant, walking calmly towards them with no reins, no rider. Just... walking on its own.

'Is it wild?' asked Charlie.

'No,' Zayed said slowly. 'Look.'

Perched on the camel's back, wings folded neatly, was a falcon, with white and silver plumage and eyes like polished onyx.

The camel came to a stop before them and knelt down with a long, groaning sigh.

'Okay, now this is really weird,' Charlie murmured.

Zayed approached the animal, palms open. He looked the camel in the eye, then turned to face the children.

'She's not wild. I think she's a spirit-helper. My grandmother spoke of them. They appear when someone is lost.'

Jemima stared at the falcon. The bird stared back. And then it nodded.

'Did it just...?' she asked in a whisper.

'Yes, it did,' said Zayed, sounding a little breathless. 'I think it knew what I said.'

Then, something happened that none of them were expecting. The falcon let out a screech, its shiny black eyes opening wide in surprise as it stared again at Jemima... or rather at the cat in her arms.

'Max,' it cried. 'Max, is that really you? Yes, it is! *Marhaba* – Hello, my friend. Look, Ghazala! Look who it is.'

The falcon looked again at Jemima. 'And it's a pleasure to meet *you* at long last, young lady. We've heard so much about you.'

'Indeed,' said Ghazala, smiling warmly at Jemima before turning to Max. 'And we said we'd meet again one day, didn't we, *Habibi* – my dear? Do you remember – *ila-liqaa* – until we meet again? That's what we told you. And here you are, back once more!'

Max nodded, his eyes growing moist as he listened to Falak and Ghazala, and he suddenly burst out with, 'Oh, my dear friends, you have no idea how happy I am to see you both again.' He didn't pause to think before he spoke, and his face split into a beaming smile.

Zayed's jaw dropped wide open. The falcon and the camel hadn't surprised him too much. He knew about spirit-helpers from the animal world, but nothing had prepared him for the sound of the cat's voice. The animal had been silent until now – he hadn't even heard it miaow. But it wasn't only *that* – these creatures already seemed to know one another. He rubbed a hand over his eyes, wondering if he was dreaming.

Jemima spotted Zayed's shocked expression and patted his arm. 'I'm sorry. We should have told you... about Max, I mean. I just wasn't sure how you'd react.'

'Is he a spirit-helper too?' asked Zayed, not taking his eyes off the cat.

'Um, no, not exactly,' she answered. 'But he can speak and understand what we say, just like they do.'

The falcon clicked his beak. 'We're old friends – Max, Ghazala, and me.'

'They saved my life,' said Max, a little shy to be speaking openly in front of Zayed. 'It's like you said – they appeared when I was lost, just when I needed them the most.'

Joe had remained silent throughout this entire exchange, his mouth hanging open as he followed the conversation. His head swung backwards and forwards between whoever was speaking, like someone watching a tennis match. Filled with remorse for the way he'd behaved towards Max, he didn't know what to say. "Sorry" would simply not be adequate. Needless to say, he felt bad about it.

'I am the Keeper of the Sands,' explained Falak. 'I'm here to guide you through the desert and to keep you safe.'

Falak then introduced Ghazala, a wise old camel and the gentlest of creatures, as Max remembered so well. She had come to carry them across the dunes and protect them from danger.

Max was immensely relieved. He'd been so ashamed that he'd told the others he knew the place they were coming to and then, when they'd arrived at the beach, it had turned out to be somewhere else entirely. He'd even begun to doubt *himself.* He'd started to wonder if Joe was right and that he'd simply dreamt his previous Arabian Adventure. That was partly why he'd remained silent – *that* and Joe being mean to him. He'd found himself sinking into a deep depression, with no inclination to speak to anyone or join in with what they were doing. Now, having met up with his two old friends again, he felt vindicated. He hadn't dreamt it or made it up. It had been real. He felt like sticking out his tongue at Joe, waggling his front paws in his ears and saying "Naah, naah!". But he resisted the urge – he wasn't a vindictive sort of cat. But he wouldn't forget it in a hurry.

That night, as they camped near a rocky outcrop, Zayed began to remember some of the stories told to him in childhood that now seemed like prophecies. He suddenly realised that their journey was mirroring an old tribal tale. Four lost souls, led by a guide – *two* guides, in their case – crossing the desert to come to the aid of a tribe in danger.

Around the campfire, Zayed told them one of the tales his grandfather used to tell – a tale of the *Sandshadows*, creatures born of loneliness and heat that stalk travellers, blending with the dunes. He'd never believed the stories until now but, here, anything seemed possible.

Later, as they lay around the embers of the fire, Joe awoke from a restless slumber and heard a faint whistling sound. He sat up and saw movement in the sand around them, like dunes shifting without any wind blowing. Eyes, reflective like insect eyes, were watching them in the darkness. 'Wake up,' he hissed. 'Something's out there.'

The others were awake in an instant, shuffling close to one another for safety.

'What is it?' asked Charlie.

'Hush! Stay quiet,' whispered Zayed. 'And don't move.'

They lay low, barely breathing until just before dawn. Only then did the shapes vanish. When they checked their surroundings, they found faint tracks – three-toed, dragging patterns – around where they'd been sleeping.

'What on earth are those?' asked Joe.

'I don't know.' Zayed traced a finger around one of the footprints. 'I can't think of any animals that make tracks like these.'

Ghazala shifted in her sleep, slowly opening her dark-lashed eyes. 'What's the matter?'

'Look at this,' said Zayed. He pointed at the marks on the ground.

Falak, who'd been dozing with his head under his wing, hopped over to take a closer look. He scratched at the prints with his claw before clicking his beak. 'Not good, not good at all. Come, we must break camp and move on.'

'But what made these?' asked Jemima, fearfully.

'Best not to ask that question for now,' replied the falcon. 'But let's be on our way. We can find another place to shelter.' He looked all around, his shrewd falcon eyes scouring the surrounding area. '*Yalla*! Come along. Hurry.'

Hearing the urgency in his voice, they quickly brushed themselves down and kicked over the embers of the fire, burying them with sand.

'Where are we going?' asked Jemima, her voice trembling with nerves.

'Somewhere a little safer,' replied Falak. 'Somewhere less open and exposed.'

'Will we have to walk far?' she asked. 'I'm so tired.'

Seeing Jemima yawn with exhaustion, Ghazala took pity on her. 'I can carry you, *Habibti* – my dear. The boys too, if you want.'

Joe and Zayed said they'd walk, but Charlie and Jemima, who was holding on to Max, gratefully accepted her offer and climbed onto the camel's back. Falak took up a perch just behind Ghazala's head.

As the camel lurched to her feet, rear end first, Jemima immediately regretted her decision, but with Zayed walking in front to guide them, Ghazala soon began to move with a smooth rhythm, as if she had walked this path a thousand times.

They plodded on through the desert in silence, eyes ever watchful, and constantly checking behind to make sure that nothing or no one was following them.

A little while later, Jemima was just nodding off, rocked by the camel's rolling gait, when the falcon suddenly took off with a loud cry.

Joe looked up, squinting as he watched the bird's frantic movements. 'Why is he circling like that?'

Zayed followed the falcon's gaze and his face turned pale. 'Oh, no! A sandstorm is coming.'

The horizon was fast vanishing behind a towering wall of dust, like a living thing rolling towards them, swallowing the sky.

'We have to find shelter!' cried Zayed. 'And fast.'

The falcon shrieked again and darted ahead. He called out something to Ghazala and the camel obeyed, lurching forward with increased speed.

They galloped up and over a ridge, and suddenly there it was – a shallow cave, hidden in the dunes. Zayed and Joe raced forward, scrambling inside just as the wind roared into life.

The storm hit like a dragon's breath – hot, dry, and furious. Sand whipped past the cave's entrance in violent gusts.

Ghazala groaned as she lay down just inside. Falak swept in after them, wings dusty and wild, and he perched on a rock. They all sat together in the narrow cave, listening to the wind howl outside.

Thanking their good fortune to have moved on from the place where they'd originally made camp, they leaned back against the rocky walls of the cave, waiting for the storm to be over.

Zayed ran his fingers over the rough stone beside him. 'Hey, what's this?'

'I think it's more symbols, like the ones at the well,' said Charlie, as he peered at the marks.

But this time there were more. Even in the

gloom of the cave, they could make out a series of ancient carvings, each one showing four figures.

'And that's a symbol of my tribe,' said Zayed, pointing at the image of an open eye surrounded by stars, etched beside the pictures.

'Wait, are those people supposed to be us?' asked Jemima, running a forefinger over the outlines. 'I can see a cat too.'

It certainly looked a little like them, but how could that be? These were ancient carvings, in a cave, in the middle of the desert.

'Stranger things have happened,' said Falak in a mysterious voice.

The children glanced at one another, not really understanding what was going on. Could it be that they were *meant* to be here – that it wasn't just by accident?

Jemima turned to Zayed. 'Do you think it was fate that we ended up here in this cave?'

He looked at her, puzzled. 'What's *fate*?'

'Like... something that's meant to happen,' she replied.

Zayed thought for a long moment. 'Maybe. Or maybe we were just lucky.'

Jemima grinned. 'Hmm, it's the same thing sometimes.'

'You are protected,' said the falcon. 'Do not ask how or by whom. Just know that your footsteps are being guided.'

'You're talking in riddles,' said Zayed. 'What does all this mean?'

'There's a dark force that is rising again,' said the falcon. 'We believe the pirates have learned of the hidden treasure beneath the desert.'

'Treasure?' said Zayed with a frown. Then he recalled the tales told since his childhood, sitting around the campfire, tales passed down from generation to generation of a place called *Atlantis of the Sands*, a lost city which lay buried in the desert – a city that was rumoured to contain an enormous hoard of treasure. 'But that's just a story, isn't it? It's not real.'

Falak didn't answer. Instead, he continued to explain. 'Listen! This is important. The pirates are led by a ruthless captain who has been searching for a treasure hidden beneath the sands. This treasure includes an ancient magic lamp – *al misbaah as-sihrii* – that has the power to summon a genie.' He glanced at Max as he spoke, knowing the cat would understand what he was saying.

At the mention of the underground treasure and the magic lamp, Max felt a sudden jolt. He knew exactly what Falak was talking about.

Zayed suddenly remembered what he'd been told, ever since he was a small child. 'Wait, I think I know something about this too,' he said. 'My family are the descendants of the ancient rulers who once protected the lamp. Is that why we're under threat from the pirates?'

'Yes, that and the treasure,' said the falcon, clicking his beak. 'They're greedy for untold wealth, as well as the power of the lamp.'

'So, what can we do to stop them?' Zayed asked.

'Perhaps there's only one solution,' answered Falak. 'And that would be to find the lamp yourselves and use its power against the pirates, to turn the tide of evil that they bring.'

Joe looked sceptical at this suggestion. 'Well, that's easier said than done, isn't it? How are we supposed to find the lamp?'

The falcon turned a knowing eye on him. 'Your feline friend could help you with that... if he felt so inclined. Max knows all about the lamp. He found it before and he can do so again.'

'Eh?' Joe's face remained blank.

'Did you listen to anything he told you, young man?' asked the falcon.

'Yes, but...'

'Yes, but nothing.' Falak snapped his beak sharply. 'Max is the wise one amongst you, despite what *you* seem to think, and you would do well to remember that. Personally, I wouldn't blame him if he was reluctant to forgive you in a hurry.'

Max had to turn his face away to hide his growing smirk when he heard the falcon put Joe in his place.

'Where will we find this place, *Atlantis of the Sands*, with the treasure and the lamp?' asked Charlie. 'Do you know the way, Max?'

'Not from here, no,' replied the cat. 'I have no idea where we are right now. But I do remember the town I was taken to and I'd recognise *that* if I saw it again.'

'So we must continue our journey?' said Zayed.

'Yes, as soon as we are able,' answered Falak, folding his wings neatly at his sides. 'For now, let's remain here.'

They stayed in the cave for the rest of the day, until the wind finally died down and the air was no longer filled with choking sand. Once the storm had passed, they were ready to set out again.

Chapter 7

Jemima, Joe, Charlie, and Zayed stood at the edge of the vast Arabian desert, their eyes squinting against the low sun as it dipped below the horizon. The air shimmered, thick with heat, and the sound of the wind whispered through the dunes like the hushed voices of ancient spirits. The sky was painted with streaks of crimson and orange, but the desert night would soon arrive, bringing with it a chill that cut through the bones.

'Are we really doing this?' Charlie asked, his voice full of hesitation.

'I guess so,' Jemima replied, her voice steady, though her heart pounded in her chest. 'There's no turning back now. We've come all this way because there's something we've got to do here. We have to see it through.'

Zayed nodded solemnly. At the age of twelve, he was just a year more than the other children, but his eyes carried the weight of someone much older.

‘I will never forgive those pirates,’ he muttered, his hands clenched into fists. ‘I must find my father before they do something terrible to him... if they haven’t already.’

‘You will,’ Jemima said, putting a hand on his shoulder. ‘And you’re not doing it alone. We're with you.’

They stood in silence for a moment, the desert stretching endlessly before them. The sun had now vanished, and the stars began to twinkle above, like a thousand eyes watching them. The full moon rose, casting its pale light across the endless sand dunes.

Suddenly, Joe’s eyes widened. ‘Did you hear that?’

The desert had been eerily quiet, save for the occasional whisper of wind. But now, a faint sound broke the silence – a distant, rhythmic drumming. It came from the far-off horizon, carried by the breeze.

Zayed’s face grew pale. ‘It’s the pirates,’ he whispered. ‘They’re on our trail.’

The falcon took to the air, calling down from above. ‘They’re still far away, but they’re getting closer.’

‘Then we need to move... fast,’ Jemima said,

a trickle of dread creeping into her gut. She looked at Joe and Charlie, then at Zayed. 'We have to make it to your tribe's camp as soon as we can.'

Zayed nodded, and without another word, he turned and led the way. Walking beside Ghazala, the three others followed, their feet sinking into the still-warm sand with each step. The wind whipped around them, carrying the scent of spices and baked earth. The desert seemed to come alive as they began their journey.

Hours passed as they trekked through the night. Jemima kept glancing over her shoulder, worried that the pirates would appear from the darkness, but the drumming sound had faded. She hoped her imagination wasn't playing tricks on her.

'Let me carry you for a while,' said Ghazala, seeing Jemima struggle.

Jemima gratefully climbed onto her back when the camel knelt down. She held Max in her arms but was so tired that she hoped she wouldn't drop him.

The moonlight cast long shadows over the dunes, turning them into towering mountains of sand. Jemima was starting to feel the weight of the journey – the fatigue, the thirst, the oppressive heat that still lingered in the air. She could feel her skin burning from the sun during the day, and now, despite the coolness of the night, exhaustion was setting in.

'Can we stop to rest?' she asked.

'Soon. We'll find somewhere safe,' Zayed replied, though his voice held an uncertainty Jemima hadn't noticed before. 'But we must be careful. The desert isn't kind to those who don't know its secrets.'

Jemima, Joe and Charlie exchanged a worried glance. What did he mean by that? Before they could ask, a gust of wind swept through the dunes, carrying a faint whisper with it – a voice that wasn't one of theirs.

'Help me...' the voice seemed to call.

They all stopped dead in their tracks. It was like the wind itself had spoken, but no one was nearby. Jemima's heart skipped a beat.

'Did you hear that?' she whispered, her voice trembling.

Zayed's face had gone ashen. 'The desert speaks in riddles,' he said, looking around nervously. 'Sometimes it warns of danger. At other times it offers help... if you can understand it.'

'But what does it mean?' asked Joe, his voice

filled with curiosity.

Before Zayed could answer, the voice returned, louder this time. 'Help me, child of the stars…'

Jemima's heart raced. Who was the child of the stars? She hadn't noticed Max freeze beside her, his ears twitching and his tail erect. For some unfathomable reason, he felt sure the voice was speaking to him.

Jemima stepped forward, instinctively following the sound, even though every part of her screamed to stop. 'What is it?' she asked, her voice barely a whisper.

Suddenly, the sands shifted beneath their feet, and the ground began to shake. The camel's ears flattened in alarm.

'It's a warning,' cried Falak. 'We must move. Now. *Yalla*.'

They barely had time to react before a shadow rose from the ground – a giant, serpentine figure, made of sand, swirling with an eerie, haunting glow. Its eyes glinted as it began to slither towards them.

Joe gasped. 'What *is* that… *thing*?'

'A sand djinn,' Falak explained in a low voice. 'They're born from the desert's magic, neither good nor evil. But they can be dangerous if they sense intruders or trespassers.'

The sand djinn's form twisted and writhed, its enormous head towering over them. Jemima could feel its gaze, heavy and piercing, like it could see into her very soul.

A voice echoed from the djinn. 'Do not fear. I am but a guardian of the desert's secrets. You seek the city of the ancients, yes? You must beware, for the pirates will not be the only ones who stand in your way. The treasure you seek is cursed.'

Zayed took a step back. 'What do you mean? We're just trying to save my father.'

The djinn's glowing eyes flickered. 'The curse will claim all who seek what lies beneath the city. But if you are brave enough, if your hearts are pure, you may yet escape it.'

The djinn's form began to fade, the swirling sands dissipating into the air like mist. 'Go... but beware the shifting sands,' it warned, its voice echoing through the desert like a distant memory.

And then, just as suddenly as it had appeared, the djinn was gone.

Jemima stood frozen, her mind racing. What had just happened? Had they really encountered a djinn?

'We must keep moving,' Falak said urgently. 'The djinn has spoken. We're on the right path, but the desert is not forgiving.'

Jemima nodded, trying to shake off the unsettling feeling the encounter had left in her gut. 'Let's go, then,' she said, trying to sound confident. But deep down, she couldn't help but wonder if they were truly ready for what lay ahead.

Chapter 8

The next morning, the desert seemed endless. The sun had already begun its ascent in the sky, casting a merciless heat over the land. The four children continued their trek, the weight of the previous night's encounter with the djinn heavy on their minds.

Jemima could hear the whispers on the breeze, as if the desert itself was speaking to them, warning them of the dangers ahead.

As they rounded a corner, the wind picked up, swirling around them in a frenzy. It seemed to have a life of its own, tugging at their clothes, murmuring strange, incomprehensible words. Jemima felt sure she could almost make out a voice calling her name, but when she turned, there was no one there.

Falak was circling overheard, scanning the horizon. The falcon suddenly let out a cry and swooped back down to join them. 'Stand still,' he whispered.

Zayed stopped, motioning for them all to be silent. Just ahead, a group of large, white creatures appeared from the haze of the desert – a herd of oryx, their long, elegant horns glinting in the sunlight.

Jemima gasped at the sight of the beautiful animals. They were magnificent, their pale coats blending with the sand around them. Their horns curved like spirals, almost shimmering in the sun. They moved with an ethereal grace, as though they were part of the very fabric of the desert itself.

'Look,' Zayed whispered. 'Those are oryx. They are the guardians of the desert. The ancestors of the unicorns.'

Jemima blinked in surprise. 'But unicorns aren't real, are they?' She looked at the large antelopes again, her eyes shining in wonder.

Zayed nodded slowly, his eyes wide with reverence. 'But *these* are real, and legends speak of the oryx as the origin of unicorns. Long ago, the people believed that the oryx were magical creatures, connected to the gods themselves. Some say the horns of the oryx are imbued with the power of the stars – an ancient magic that can only be unlocked by those who are pure of heart.'

Joe squinted, watching the mystical

creatures. 'D'you think they'll help us?'

Ghazala shook her head. 'As beautiful as they might look, the oryx are not to be trusted lightly. They're creatures of the desert, not of men. But perhaps they will guide us for a while.'

As if in response to the camel's words, one of the oryx turned its head towards them, its dark eyes locking with Jemima's. The desert wind seemed to pause for a moment, holding its breath, before the creature began to move in their direction.

A soft, melodic sound echoed through the dunes like a distant bell, or the chime of an ancient temple. Jemima felt it resonate within her chest, a strange warmth spreading through her. She took a step forward, her body moving almost of its own accord.

The oryx came closer, its hooves making no sound on the sand. Its eyes never left Jemima's and, as it stopped just a few paces away, Jemima felt a wave of understanding wash over her. The creature was offering something – something ancient, something powerful. Then it looked at the cat held in her arms and made a soft sound, almost like a greeting.

Without thinking, Jemima reached out, her

hand brushing against the oryx's horn. A jolt of energy shot through her, and she stumbled back, her heart racing. The horn was cold, impossibly cold, but the magic that emanated from it was undeniable. It was the same energy she'd felt when they first arrived in the desert, and when the djinn had warned them of the treasure's curse.

'It says the desert is alive,' Jemima whispered, her voice filled with awe. 'I think it's trying to show us something.'

Zayed nodded, his face pale. 'The desert is full of secrets. The oryx are the keepers of those secrets. If they *are* guiding us, we may be closer to finding the truth.'

Joe, his curiosity piqued, stepped forward. 'So, the legends of unicorns came from these antelopes?' He'd always thought they were just make-believe.

Zayed's eyes darkened. 'The ancient people believed that the oryx were a manifestation of the gods. And that those who followed the oryx were blessed with the power to find what was hidden in the desert – maybe the treasure beneath the city?'

'I think they're bringing us a warning,' said Jemima, looking one of them in the eye. It seemed to be trying to say something to her. Then she heard it – a clear message flashed into her head, not spoken words, but she understood it all the same. 'It's telling us to beware. That many who seek the treasure never return.'

As Jemima gazed at the oryx, she couldn't shake off the feeling that their journey was about to take a darker turn. The desert was a place of mystery and magic, but it was also a place of danger where ancient forces were at play, and no one, not even the beautiful oryx, could be trusted completely.

'I think we need to move on now,' Jemima said softly. 'We've been given a warning, but I'm not sure what it means.'

Zayed turned to look at her, his face full of determination. 'The oryx have spoken. We must follow them, or we'll lose our way. Am I right, Falak?'

The falcon nodded. 'We can let them lead us... for a while at least.'

The herd of oryx began to move, their graceful bodies gliding across the dunes like pale shadows. They all followed, hearing the eerie chimes of the oryx's call echo in the wind. But as they moved deeper into the desert, the air grew heavy with a sense of foreboding.

There was something in the desert that was watching them – a primeval presence, far older than the city they were seeking. And though the oryx were showing them the way, Jemima couldn't help thinking they were walking into something far more sinister than they'd ever imagined.

The treasure, the pirates, the curse – it was all leading to something. But what? Their journey was far from over. And the desert, with all its mysteries, had only just begun to reveal its secrets.

Every now and again the oryx checked that the group of travellers was still behind them. Following the herd, they arrived at a stand of palms beside a small watering hole where the animals made it clear it was time to rest for a while.

Ghazala slurped noisily, drinking her fill before lowering herself onto the sand under the trees. The children settled down beside her, glad of the shade from the punishing glare of the sun. Falak joined them but kept a constant watchful eye on the surrounding dunes.

'Zayed,' Jemima whispered, her voice barely audible. 'Where are the oryx taking us?'

Zayed was silent for a moment, his eyes scanning the horizon. 'I'm not sure, but I believe the oryx know more than we do,' he said quietly.

“They’ve watched over this land for centuries. But not everything they know is meant to be shared with others. I only hope we can trust them.’

Falak and Ghazala agreed with him, knowing that it paid to be wary.

As dusk began to fall, the oryx grew restless, making their strange musical calls to one another. They were ready to set off again.

The desert stretched out before them like a never-ending sea of sand. The moon had climbed higher into the night sky, casting its cold silver light across the dunes. The children followed the oryx as they glided through the barren landscape, their soft hooves making no sound. The creatures’ curved horns caught the moonlight, glowing faintly as if enchanted. The air was thick with the scent of ancient dust and forgotten history.

But even the guiding presence of the majestic creatures of the desert wasn’t enough to dispel the feeling of danger that hung in the air. The silence was too heavy, too watchful. Jemima felt sure they were being followed – although every time she glanced back, there was nothing but the wind stirring the sand.

After walking at a steady pace for a couple of hours, they paused again. Seated in a circle, the children shared a handful of dates and a few sips from their clay pot which they'd filled at the watering hole.

'Hey, where are they?' Joe asked suddenly, looking over his shoulder. 'They've gone.'

They all turned around to see. He was right. The herd of oryx had moved silently away and were now far off in the distance, their pale coats glowing silver in the moonlight.

'Why have they left us all alone?' asked Jemima, sounding panicky as she watched them disappear over the shadowy dunes. 'What if we can't find our way from here?'

'They must have their reasons,' said Zayed. 'But we're not alone – we have Falak and Ghazala.'

The falcon and the camel both nodded. 'You are safe with us. We will not leave you,' said Falak.

Chapter 9

They set out again with the moon still above them. The falcon flew ahead, leading them past forgotten wells and tracks through the dunes, until finally, in the distance, the faint glow of lanterns appeared – dozens of them, moving slowly across the sands.

'A caravan,' Zayed whispered. 'Traders.'

They approached cautiously. Merchants with long robes and curved swords watched as the children drew near, but when Zayed told his story in rapid Arabic, a tall man with a dark blue sash nodded.

'You can travel with us,' he said. 'You are under *kafala* – our protection – now.'

Jemima sagged with relief. They were safe. 'Finally. Something good,' she said. 'Real people – not desert spirits.'

The caravan moved silently beneath the moon, dozens of camels swaying in rhythm, their loads tied with ropes that creaked softly. Jemima, Charlie and Max rode on Ghazala's back. Zayed and Joe rode beside them, eyes alert, while the falcon glided overhead like a silent guardian.

They should have been feeling safe now that they were with the traders, but a sense of unease clung to the darkness around them, and they still felt that someone or some*thing* was out there, watching them.

For the next two days, the caravan pushed deeper and deeper into the desert, navigating by the stars at night and following ancient trails.

Every now and again, when they stopped to rest, they came across large stones, etched with mystical carvings, similar to the ones the children had seen at the well and in the cave.

Up and down over the towering dunes they trekked, the camels plodding easily over the soft sand with their large, spongey feet.

The merchants were horrified that the children were so badly prepared for the harsh conditions of their journey. They dug into their packs of merchandise and brought out light robes and lengths of fabric.

'Here, wrap these scarves around your heads and faces to protect you from the sun. Leave only your eyes visible,' said one of the men. 'And wrap some cloth around your feet against the burning heat. It will help.'

To these kind gifts, others also added waterskins. 'How can you travel through the desert without drinking water?' asked one of them, tutting in disbelief.

Along the way, the traders explained how to use the stars to orientate themselves at night and how to recognise which desert plants held moisture if they were short of water.

'All these things are vital for survival when you undertake a journey such as this,' the merchants explained.

Overwhelmed by their generosity, Jemima thanked them profusely. 'We're so grateful for your help and, honestly, I feel so much better now my skin is covered up,' she said. 'We couldn't have carried on like that for much longer. In fact, I don't know how we made it this far.'

'And nor do we,' said the leader of the caravan. 'It was fortunate that you found us... or I dread to think what might have happened to you.'

As the sun sank down over the horizon, the caravan halted and the merchants made camp as usual, with the camels forming a protective circle around them. The men rigged up canopies overhead and, with blankets spread on the ground, it was time to grab a few hours' rest.

With the dazzling sunset already beginning to fade, the children lay close to one another, talking quietly as they watched the sparks from the campfire shoot heavenwards.

'Don't move,' Zayed cried suddenly, placing a restraining hand on Charlie's shoulder.

A scorpion, the size of Charlie's hand, crawled across the sand in front of them. Its tail arched like a hooked blade, and its black body shimmered in the firelight.

'Stay still,' Zayed warned. 'They hunt by movement.'

Charlie's breath caught in his throat. The scorpion paused, then continued past, vanishing into the rocks.

Charlie exhaled slowly, his panic subsiding. 'I really wasn't made for this place,' he said, shakily. 'Desert living isn't my kind of thing.'

Zayed gave him a faint smile. 'Don't worry. You're doing okay.'

But, as the sun rose the next morning, bathing the sky in a pale orange glow, they awoke to bad news.

The traders were heading off along a different route and told the children they must continue their journey alone.

'The trail that you're following will take you deeper into the Empty Quarter, but we're not going that way,' said the leader of the caravan. 'You must beware. There are whispers of sand vipers beyond the *wadi* – the dried river. That place is cursed.'

Jemima swallowed hard. 'Are they real? The vipers?'

'Yes, they're real,' said Zayed. 'And silent. They hide beneath the sand, so be careful of where you tread. Their bite can kill before the sun sets.'

When he heard this, Max clung to Jemima. 'Don't put me down on the ground,' he pleaded. 'You know how I feel about snakes.'

Parting from the traders with heavy hearts, they continued alone, following the falcon's shadow as he swept ahead. The heat swelled, merciless. Sweat clung to their backs. Even Ghazala seemed weary.

Within a couple of hours, Charlie staggered and then fell to his knees.

'I need water,' he said, his voice dry and cracking.

'Soon,' Zayed promised. 'We're close to a place where we can fill our water skins.'

And then, like a mirage made real, it

appeared. A grove of palms, swaying over a glistening pool of water, half-hidden between two sand-covered hills. Birds darted between the trees. Flowers bloomed like forgotten jewels.

'It's a proper oasis,' Jemima whispered. 'Look! It's so beautiful.'

They all ran forward, falling to their knees at the water's edge. The camel drank noisily. The falcon dipped its wings in the pool, flicking droplets into the air, before gulping down beakfuls of the precious liquid.

Then, they all rested in the shade, eating dates and sweet pomegranates from the trees, waiting for the fierce afternoon heat to subside. As the sun dipped lower behind the dunes, the children lay under the swaying palms, their bellies full and their limbs heavy with exhaustion.

Only Zayed stayed awake, staring at the pool, his thoughts turning over like stones in a rippling stream. The pearl hidden deep in his woven bag pressed against his side like a secret that grew heavier with every passing hour.

'We must make it back to my tribe. I need to tell them what's happened to my father,' he murmured under his breath, his eyes full of sorrow. 'I hope he's still alive.... that the pirates haven't killed him.' His voice cracked, and he quickly dashed a hand across his eyes to swipe away the tears that threatened to fall.

'Tsk, tsk,' said Falak, perched high above them in one of the palm trees. 'They will not kill him, Zayed. They need him.'

'For the ransom money?' Zayed peered up at the falcon, shielding his eyes against the sun.

'Maybe, maybe. But they also think he can lead them to the hidden city.'

'How? Does he know where it is?' asked Zayed. 'Because, if he does, he's never told me.'

Falak ruffled his feathers, fluttering down to perch beside the boy. 'He may not have told you, but your father *knows*. The pirates will press him, and he will resist... for a time.'

Zayed scowled. 'Why would he keep that from me? I'm his son.'

'Some secrets are buried to protect the ones we love,' Falak replied, tilting his head. 'Especially when danger stirs beneath the sand.'

Jemima sat up, brushing sand from her face. 'What kind of danger? More vipers?'

The falcon's eyes gleamed. 'Worse. There are things that slither beneath even the vipers. Shadows with no names. The kind of things that wake when too many speak of treasure and lost cities.'

Charlie turned over with a groan. 'Well, now I'm definitely not sleeping.' He pushed himself up onto his elbows, glancing nervously around him.

'No. You must all sleep for a little longer,' urged Falak. 'You need to be strong for what lies ahead.'

Sleep came, drawn by the long journey and the safety of the oasis. One by one, they drifted off as the stars appeared... until the whispering began.

Max was the first to stir. Wary, the cat's ears twitched, his tail fluffing out. He rose slowly, back arched, eyes glowing in the moonlight.

Jemima opened her eyelids, sensing his unease. 'What is it, Max?'

Before he could answer, a gust of wind swept through the palms, extinguishing the small fire they'd built. The air thickened, heavy with heat and something else – a *presence.*

And then she appeared. She rose from the pool like steam, her form shrouded in a silvery mist. A woman, and yet not a woman. Her eyes glowed violet, and her voice echoed not in their ears, but in their minds.

'Why have you come to my sanctuary?'

Zayed scrambled to his feet, instinctively placing himself between the spirit and the others. 'I'm sorry. We didn't know – please, we meant no harm.'

The woman's eyes flicked towards him. 'You carry something that calls to the deep places. A pearl, shaped by time and grief.'

Charlie blinked. 'Excuse me, are you... a-are you a *djinn*?'

The spirit did not smile, but her eyes gleamed. 'Yes, but I am also a warning.'

Max hissed softly. 'Warnings don't usually show up in the middle of nowhere with glowing eyes.'

'Silence, Familiar,' she said. 'Be still.'

Max turned as stiff as a board, eyes wide with surprise when he found he couldn't move or speak.

Jemima stepped forward. 'Please – we just want to help Zayed find his tribe. His father's been taken by pirates. We're not after treasure and we don't know anything about a pearl.'

The djinn tilted her head. 'But the treasure is calling you. It listens. It *remembers*. The pearl is a key. And keys open doors that are best left shut.'

Falak swooped down, wings outstretched.

‘*Halass*! Enough riddles! Speak plainly. What danger lies ahead?’ he asked.

The djinn raised a hand, and the pool behind her began to shimmer and shift. Images danced upon the water’s surface – a vast stone gate buried beneath sand, flanked by statues with glowing eyes. A chained man stood before it, head bowed. Around him, shadows moved, figures cloaked in black, their blades glinting.

‘This is your future, unless you turn back now,’ said the djinn. ‘The city you seek is a city no more. It hides more than treasure and its door must remain sealed. There is a curse…’

Zayed stared at the vision, his fists clenched. ‘But that man in chains is my father…’

‘If you go forward,’ she said, her voice softening, ‘you may save him. But you may lose much more.’

The pool stilled. The djinn’s body faded into mist, then vanished entirely, leaving behind only silence.

Jemima felt the chill linger in the air. ‘Oh my. What do we do now?’

Zayed didn’t answer right away. His gaze was fixed on the spot where the vision had been. Then, quietly, he said, ‘We keep going.’

Max let out a long breath, finally able to move again. ‘Of course we do, because it wouldn’t be a proper adventure without a curse and a prophecy or two, would it?’ he said in a sarcastic tone of voice. ‘Oh, why does this always happen to us?’

Charlie rubbed his eyes. ‘Can’t we just have *one* normal day for once?’

The falcon took to the air once more. ‘Come dawn, we move. The djinn’s warning was clear. But she only said “*may*”, remember? Nothing is certain.’

Zayed’s voice remained firm. ‘We’re not turning back.’

And although no one spoke it aloud, they all knew that the hardest part of the journey had only just begun.

Chapter 10

By morning, the oasis had changed. Gone was the peaceful shimmer of the pool, the cheerful chatter of birds in the palms. The air was tight with tension, and the trees swayed more than they should in the still heat. None of them spoke of the djinn – not directly – but the echo of her warning hung in the air.

They set out early, before the sun's full fury could descend, following Falak as he glided above the dunes. The falcon led them south-west, away from the comfort of the oasis, towards a strip of land where the sand had darkened and flattened into cracked, silvery earth.

Zayed halted at the top of a dune and pointed. 'That's it. The wadi. The dried riverbed. The traders call it the *Path of Venom and Doom*.'

Max immediately jumped into Jemima's arms. 'No. Nope. No, thank you. I'm allergic to venom – all snakes, in fact. And dried rivers. And, um, doom.'

Charlie squinted ahead, shielding his eyes from the sun. He wished he'd brought his sunglasses from home. 'Um, it doesn't look so bad.'

'Exactly,' Zayed said grimly. 'That's what makes it dangerous.'

They descended slowly, Ghazala's careful steps sinking into the softer sand. The wadi spread before them like a scar, twisting through the desert, littered with ancient bones, large stones, and brittle reeds.

'Stay close,' said Zayed. 'And step where I step. The vipers don't chase. They lie in wait beneath the surface. If we disturb the sand the wrong way...'

He didn't need to finish. Max whimpered and hid his face in Jemima's scarf.

They walked in single file. Zayed led the way, scanning the ground with each step. Falak circled above, watching from the sky. The others followed in silence, even Max. He was too tense to complain. Ghazala brought up the rear.

The heat shimmered off the cracked earth, distorting the horizon. Wind whispered through the dry reeds, making them rustle and chatter like living creatures. A single bird shrieked and vanished into the blue.

Jemima's eyes darted constantly around, searching for movement. Her heart pounded. Every shadow looked like a coiled snake. Every crunch beneath their shoes could be the start of something deadly.

Halfway across the dried-up riverbed, Zayed raised a hand. 'Stop!'

They all froze in their tracks.

Then they heard it – *a hiss*. As soft as sand trickling through fingers.

Zayed pointed ahead. A long slit had appeared in the earth. Something pale and scaly was disappearing back underneath the surface.

'There's one,' whispered Zayed. 'That was close.'

Charlie wiped the sweat from his brow. 'But that thing was *huge*. I thought vipers aren't supposed to be big.'

'They grow large here... and old.' Zayed's face was tense. 'We need to move faster.'

They kept going, hearts thudding. A cloud passed over the sun, casting the riverbed into eerie shadow. Then...

'Careful!' yowled Max.

Charlie had stumbled. His foot slipped, kicking up a spray of sand. Jemima lunged and caught his arm, pulling him back just as the ground shifted. It looked like something was rising beneath it.

A pale-scaled serpent suddenly burst from the sand, twice as long as Charlie's leg. Its body glistened like oil. As it reared up, its mouth opened to reveal two long fangs.

Before anyone could even utter a scream, Falak dived down from the sky.

The falcon struck the viper mid-lunge, slamming it sideways. The snake hissed furiously and thrashed in the sand, but Falak wheeled again, talons flashing.

With a shout, Zayed hurled a stone and the creature, dazed and injured, slithered back into its hole, disappearing beneath the surface.

A shocked silence followed, apart from the sound of everyone breathing hard.

'It's okay. I'm all right,' Charlie managed to force out in a shaky voice. 'I didn't get bitten.'

'But you *almost* did,' said Joe. 'And if something happened to you, how would I explain that to your mum?' He gave his friend a rueful grin, but his taut, white face betrayed the fear he'd felt.

Jemima let out a long breath, her heart thumping against her ribcage. 'Let's just... keep moving and hope there aren't more of them.'

'*Shway, shway* – slowly,' said Zayed.

Following his instructions, they continued across the *wadi* at a slower pace. More cautious now, they walked like ghosts, trying to step as lightly as possible, so as not to disturb anything beneath the surface. They spoke in low whispers, hardly daring to make a sound. When, at last, they stepped off the cracked riverbed and back onto stable sand, they collapsed in relief.

'We made it,' said Zayed. 'That was the worst part and it's over.'

Falak flapped his wings as he swooped down to perch on Ghazala's back. 'No, it's not the worst part. Not yet. But it *is* over.'

Jemima turned, looking back with a shudder at the wadi stretching behind them. The sun had burned away the shadows, but the memory of that hiss lingered like a painful bruise.

'What now?' she asked.

Zayed pointed to the horizon. In the distance, dark hills rose like broken teeth from the desert floor.

'I think those mark the edge of the Great Plateau,' he said. 'If I'm right, my tribe's lands begin just beyond it.'

Charlie groaned. 'That sounds like code for "more climbing" if you ask me.'

'And maybe worse,' added Falak. 'There are *watchers* in the hills.'

'Watchers?' repeated Jemima.

But Falak was already soaring off into the sky again and didn't answer.

Whatever lay ahead, they were one step closer to the truth. And one step closer to the pirates who held Zayed's father.

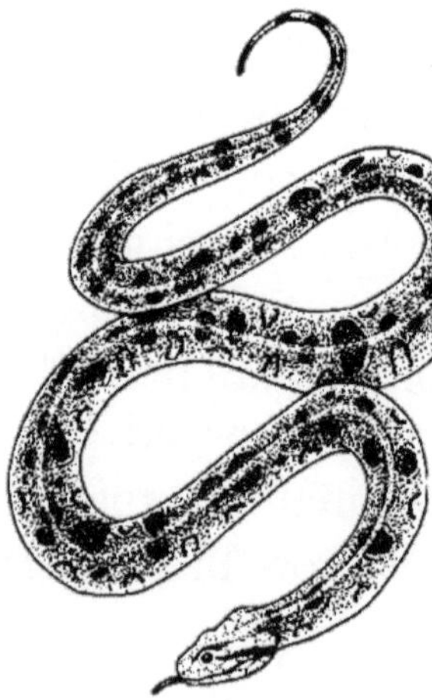

Chapter 11

The hills were not what the children had expected. From a distance, they'd looked like stone — solid, dry, dead. But up close, the land seemed to be alive. Caves opened like mouths in the rock. Strange plants, wiry and sharp, grew in twisted patches between slabs of sandstone. The air smelled faintly of ash and something sweeter... like rotting fruit.

Falak flew low, wings twitching. 'Something is wrong. I can feel it,' he said.

They moved cautiously, weaving through narrow gullies and over ridges baked hot by the sun. Ghazala snorted and refused to step near a cluster of jagged rocks. Her ears flattened, and she tossed her head nervously.

'She doesn't like it here,' Zayed murmured, rubbing the camel's flank.

'I don't,' said the camel. 'There's something bad in the air. I don't want to go any further.'

Max's tail fluffed out like a plume. 'I second Ghazala. Let's go back to the cursed snake riverbed.

Even that place felt friendlier than here.'

'I'm watching for movement,' said Joe, gripping a rock for support as they climbed. 'I don't see anything yet.'

But Jemima was frowning at the ground. 'It's *too* quiet,' she commented. 'No birds, no insects. Not even a breeze.'

Then she saw it — a set of tracks in the dust. Long. Claw-like. Not quite human. She pointed. 'What made *those*?'

Zayed crouched down to take a closer look. 'I've never seen prints like these before.'

Max hopped down and sniffed the edge of a footprint. 'Something tall and heavy. And it doesn't wear shoes. What kind of creature leaves tracks like this?'

Charlie cleared his throat. 'Uh... guys?' His eyes were fixed on a spot above them.

They all turned, following his gaze.

High up on a rocky ledge, silhouetted by the sun, *something* was watching them.

It was tall, at least the size of a man, but impossibly thin — like skin wrapped tight over a skeleton. Its face was a mask of cracked earth, its eyes round and dark, like polished stones. Then it vanished, sliding backwards into the shadows.

Zayed stepped back in alarm. 'That was a Sandshadow.'

'A *what*?' asked Joe, his voice sounding higher than usual.

'They're not supposed to be real,' Zayed said. 'I've heard about them, but only in stories that my tribe tells. They're spirits of the desert, cursed to guard old secrets. But they only appear near sacred places.'

Jemima's stomach dropped. 'Perhaps that means we're close.'

Falak landed on a nearby rock. 'Or that maybe we've gone too far.'

They climbed faster, nerves on edge, eyes scanning every shadow. At the top of the next ridge, they paused... and saw dozens of the strange tracks leading into a narrow gorge between two cliffs.

'There's no other way through,' said Zayed. 'We have to go down there.'

Max shuddered. 'I hate narrow places. That's where *things* hide – like scorpions and snakes and rats... and other *things*.'

Still, they descended, rocks shifting underfoot. The walls of the gorge rose around them, blocking out the sun. The temperature dropped. Shadows stretched long. Halfway through, the wind shifted, and the whispering began.

It wasn't in any language they knew. Just breathy syllables and sighs, echoing around the stone. The air felt thick and heavy, pressing them in, weighing them down.

Charlie froze. 'Something's up ahead.'

Jemima shuffled forward. Around the bend, the gorge opened into a round hollow... and at its centre stood a ring of ancient stones, each one carved with similar symbols to the others they'd seen before. But more disturbing were the statues – five of them, arranged in a circle. Tall, thin, and hunched, they were stone versions of the Sandshadows they'd seen before. But these were broken – cracked open at the chest.

Max crept closer and sniffed at the one closest to him. 'Um... I don't think these are statues, actually.'

'What do you mean?' asked Zayed.

'I mean that they used to be alive,' replied the spooked cat, his whiskers twitching.

Jemima leapt backwards in fright. 'Alive? Falak, what is this place?'

The falcon didn't answer. He was staring at

the soft bag slung across Zayed's chest. It seemed to bulge, and he could see the outline of something round, glowing faintly through the woven rushes it was made from.

Then, a scraping sound behind made them all whirl around. They turned in time to see a Sandshadow step out of the stone wall of the gorge, seeping like smoke from cracks in the rock. Then another. And another. They were surrounded.

Falak let out a sharp cry. 'Do not run. Do not let them see fear.'

Zayed stepped forward, trembling but steady. 'We haven't come to steal anything. We're just trying to find my father. That's all.'

The Sandshadows stood still. Then the closest one raised an arm and pointed a long, spindly finger directly at Zayed's bag.

'What does it want?' whispered Jemima, quaking with terror at the sight of these beings.

'Something I have,' he answered in a low voice. 'Something I haven't told you about.'

'Is it the pearl?' she asked with a frown. 'The one the Djinn mentioned?'

He nodded miserably. 'They know what it is. I should have told you.'

As he spoke, the ground trembled. Cracks

spidered across the earth beneath their feet, circling the stone ring. Suddenly, the centre of the circle collapsed, leaving a large round hole at its heart and a staircase that spiralled down into the dark.

The Sandshadows moved aside, watching in silence, waiting to see what he did next.

Zayed was tempted. He took a step forward, then hesitated. No, this didn't feel right. It was a trap, he was sure of it. 'What should I do?' he asked Falak.

'You've been given a choice, Zayed, but you know the answer in your heart,' replied the falcon.

Zayed looked once more at the dark chasm open before him. He felt it pulling him towards the staircase. Who knew where it might lead? Then, with a backward glance at his new friends, he saw they were all shaking their heads. Taking a deep breath, he stepped back from the abyss.

'Come on, *yalla* – let's go,' he said, turning on his heel. 'We need to get away from here.'

Breathing a huge sigh of relief, they followed him as he set off again, keen to escape the claustrophobic atmosphere of the gorge.

As the children hurried away, the Sandshadows melted back into the rockface with a long hiss of air, like the sound of a deflating balloon.

The children emerged from the ravine just as the sky turned silver with early dawn. Before them stretched another endless plain of dunes.

At that moment, the falcon called out a warning and they all looked up, trying to see what it had spotted. Falak cried out again, sharper this time, more urgent.

Zayed turned his head slowly towards the dunes. A small glint of something metal caught his eye, then a flicker of shadow. 'Oh, no, I think it's the pirates,' he whispered. 'They've found us.'

'What are we going to do?' asked Charlie.

'Let's all sit on Ghazala's back, and she can gallop far away from here,' suggested Joe.

'But they'll just follow us,' Zayed murmured. 'They won't stop. Not now.'

Joe glanced back but saw nothing. The dunes were empty. 'So what do we do? Wait for them to catch us?'

'We go where they will not,' Zayed said. 'A place only my people know. It's dangerous – but I've heard that the pirates fear the desert's teeth.'

Charlie wasn't sure if that was just a metaphor or something that was actually real, until just before dawn, when they stopped near a jagged outcrop of rocks which resembled an open jaw. Then he understood.

The wind sighed, whispering between the fang-like stones. It sounded just like the voice they'd heard before.

'Turn back... the path is guarded,' it warned.

'What's that?' asked Jemima, pointing towards a jagged shape that jutted from a nearby rise, its dark silhouette slumped sideways like a fallen giant.

'Looks like a collapsed building,' said Charlie. 'Or, at least, what's left of one.'

They climbed towards it, their feet sinking in the sand. Ghazala paused to shake dust from her back. Falak circled once, then landed on a cracked pillar. The wind howled softly through holes in the stone.

'This was once a watchtower,' said Zayed, as they neared the heap of stones that lay half-buried in the sand. 'Built by desert guardians – people who protected trade routes and sacred paths.'

Max leapt down from Jemima's arms and sniffed the air. 'I've seen something like this before. Wait, let me think for a moment.' He blinked and turned, staring at the base of the tower where sand had piled up around the collapsed wall.

'It was on a map. Remember me telling you about when I first came here and was in the magician's house? During the night, I had a snoop around the room where I slept and I found a dusty old scroll he'd left on the table. I'm pretty sure this tower was drawn on it.'

Joe raised an eyebrow. 'Are you trying to say you remember a map from ages ago that you only saw once?'

Max didn't even look at him. 'I have a cat's memory, Joe. It's perfect. Unlike yours.'

The children moved closer. Carved into the wall, half-hidden beneath the sand, were sun, moon, and star symbols, like so many of the others they'd seen along the way. Zayed brushed it clean, revealing a series of etched lines leading away from the tower like rays.

Charlie traced them with his fingers. 'They look like roads.'

'That's right. I think they're routes through the desert,' murmured Zayed.

Max nodded, remembering the magician's map. 'Yes. This one leads to a place called the Whispering Dunes.' He pointed with his paw.

'That's where the gate to the lost city is supposed to be, according to the drawing on the scroll I saw.' Despite what he'd said to Joe, Max himself was amazed that he could remember all this in so much detail.

Zayed stood up straighter. 'Then, this is the route we must follow. If we can reach the city before the pirates, we'll have the advantage.'

Charlie gave a hollow laugh. 'Yeah, if you call entering an ancient, cursed ruin with vipers, sand spirits, and bloodthirsty pirates chasing us as having an *advantage*.'

But they didn't turn back.

The wind had changed. There was now a heaviness to it, as if the desert itself was struggling to breathe.

They kept going for the next few hours, following the route carved on the stone. The sand grew finer, the air hotter. At midday they stopped in the shade of a narrow ravine to rest for a while.

As they drank sparingly from their water skins, Falak let out a sharp warning cry from overhead.

They turned and saw a lone figure approaching across the sands – cloaked, limping, leaning on a staff. He waved to them.

'Help!' he called. 'Please. I've been robbed. Traders attacked me and took my camel.'

'Oh, poor man,' exclaimed Jemima. 'That's terrible. We must help him.'

Charlie narrowed his eyes. 'Wait! Do you believe him? That feels suspiciously... convenient.'

Zayed hesitated. 'I suppose it *could* be true. There are bandits out here.'

Max padded ahead slowly, his nostrils twitching.

The man stumbled closer. He looked ragged, with a sunburnt face and trembling hands. 'I've been walking for days. I... I know this area, though. If you're lost, I can guide you. There's an old temple to the north with fresh water and shade. You can rest there before you cross into the Whispering Dunes.'

Max now walked in a slow circle around him, tail stiff and upright. He sniffed deeply. 'That's a bit odd,' he murmured. 'Your clothes smell of sea salt.'

The man's eyes flicked to Max. Just for a moment. Then he moved fast, no longer hunched over and limping. He grabbed Zayed's bag.

'You have the pearl. Give it to me!' he rasped.

But Zayed was quicker. He twisted away as Jemima lunged forward and Joe grabbed a handful of the man's cloak. They tumbled together, kicking up sand. The man hissed and, scrambling to his feet, struck Joe across the face, before turning to run away. But he chose the wrong direction. He raced towards what looked like a smooth patch of sand, but Zayed's warning came too late.

'No! Watch out! That's quicksand,' Zayed called.

The man shrieked in panic as his foot sank. Then his leg. Then both. The more he struggled, the faster he sank.

'Throw me the pearl!' he yelled, reaching out with one free arm. 'They'll come for it! You don't know what you're carrying.'

Zayed stood still, watching him sink, his face unreadable. Jemima's heart pounded, but no one moved to help. The sand swallowed the stranger with a long, sucking hiss. Then, silence.

Charlie wiped his face. His hands were shaking. 'The guy might have been one of the baddies, but that was still a horrible thing to see,' he said. '*Horrible.*'

'Well, we know for certain now that they're tracking us,' said Joe.

Zayed nodded. 'And it sounds like they know where we're going.'

'They'll follow,' said the falcon. 'And next time, it won't be just *one* man. It'll be the whole crew.'

Joe turned to the others, his voice steady, despite the fact that his face still stung from the blow he'd received. 'Then we have to find the city *first*. Get to the lamp. Get answers. And be ready for what's waiting.'

'Yes, we have to find the lamp,' Jemima said quietly. 'It's the only way to protect the pearl. And save your father, Zayed.'

He nodded, his gaze distant. 'He's holding out, I'm sure of it. But the pirates won't wait forever. *Yanni* – y'know, it's time I told you about this...'

They all looked as Zayed reached into his woven bag and drew out the pearl.

Wide-eyed, the children stared at the large, lustrous sphere. It was almost as if there was light trapped inside it, making it glow like a full moon. It was clear to see this was no ordinary pearl.

'Oh, my goodness,' breathed Jemima. 'I've never seen anything like that before. No wonder the pirates want to get their hands on it.'

'How's it glowing like that?' asked Charlie.

'I don't know,' said Zayed. 'I thought it was just a pearl – now I'm not so sure. I think it must contain some kind of magic, if that doesn't sound too silly.'

'After everything else we've experienced, it doesn't sound silly at all,' said Jemima.

'I'm sorry I haven't told you about it before now,' he continued. 'It's not that I don't trust you, but my father said I had to keep it safe at all costs. I figured the fewer people who knew about it the better.'

'That's okay,' she replied. 'We understand. There's things we haven't told you either.' She looked at Joe and Charlie before continuing. 'Maybe now's the time for all of us to be honest with one another.'

At a nod from the two boys, she explained it all, telling Zayed about their missing parents, the old book that was their gateway into the past, the special key, the magic golden owl charms which made it possible to speak and understand any language wherever they went, including that of animals... and finally the fact they'd come from the future – the 21st century to be exact.

When she'd finished, Zayed simply smiled.

'That explains everything. I knew there was more to your story than you were telling me. And now I understand how Max can speak and why he's been here before.'

'Most people would think we're crazy if we told them all that,' said Joe.

'Or even think we're spies,' added Charlie, remembering some of their experiences during their other trips into the past.

'Ah, but then those people might think we're *all* crazy if we tried to tell them about talking falcons and camels, not to mention some of the other things we've seen since we set out on this journey,' said Zayed.

'That's true,' said Joe. 'But perhaps we *are*? Crazy, I mean.'

They all began to laugh.

'But I'm really sorry about your parents,' said Zayed. 'I hope you find them.'

'Thanks,' replied Jemima. 'That's why we understand about your father and want to help you rescue him.'

Zayed looked at the twins, a thoughtful expression on his face. 'Based on what you've told me about your other journeys through time, do you think your parents are here in Arabia?'

Jemima realised this was the first time on an adventure that she hadn't wondered if they'd find Mum and Dad there. She didn't think they were. She couldn't sense their presence, and something told her they'd never been in this place. She was sure she'd have felt it – in her heart and in her bones – if they had. 'No, I'm pretty sure they're not,' she said with a wistful smile. 'Not this time.' And she was surprised to feel that she didn't mind.

'So, what happens next?' asked Joe.

'We keep going,' said Zayed in a determined voice. 'I think we're getting close now. My tribe camps near the ruins of an ancient town not far from here – *Iram al-'Imad* – The City of Pillars. The old ones called it *Ubar*.'

Max's ears pricked up at the name. He remembered Iram of the Pillars from his last visit. It was where the magician lived.

Charlie blinked. 'Wait, I think I've read about that place, but people think it was just a legend. Wasn't it?'

Zayed shook his head. 'No, it's a real place. But the town lies in ruins now, mostly forgotten. My people live in its shadow.'

'Hang on. Are we missing something here?' Jemima said with a puzzled frown. 'Surely there can't be *two* ancient cities in ruins near here, both lost to time? What if they're one and the same?'

'Yes,' agreed Charlie. 'You know all about the remains of Iram, or Ubar, because the ruins are on the surface, above ground – but what if there's more that you don't know about because you can't see it? The lost city might be buried underneath those ruins.'

Zayed nodded slowly. 'So, Atlantis of the Sands has been there all along, right under our noses?'

'Max told us the magician who kidnapped him rode out into the desert to find a trapdoor hidden under the sand,' said Jemima. 'But that might just have been another entrance to the city that no one else knew about. It led straight into a tunnel where there were treasure chambers. Then Max had to find a gate into a garden where the lamp was hidden.'

'So that wasn't the *main* gateway into the lost city,' said Joe. 'But it was the same place we're looking for.'

'Yeah, that makes sense,' Charlie said, thinking it through. 'So, which way should we go?'

Zayed felt the pearl vibrate as if it was trying to tell him something. He suddenly knew what they had to do. 'We make for the main gateway,' he decided. '*Yalla*! Let's go.'

They set off, moving with a renewed sense of purpose.

The wind grew restless once more, as if sensing what lay ahead. And, as the sun began to dip, they saw it. In the distance, crumbling towers rose from the dunes. Half-buried columns reclaimed by the desert and walls carved with symbols so ancient that they'd been eroded by the wind, by sand, and by time itself.

Chapter 12

After Zayed's escape from the dhow, the pirates had taken his father to their ship. Khaled had watched his son dive deep beneath the waves where he was soon lost from sight. He had no idea what had happened to the boy and prayed that he'd made it to safety with the pearl.

With the salty scent of brine and the metallic tang of blood in the air, the pirates had dragged Khaled across the deck of the *Scorpion's Smile*. He was no ordinary prisoner. Khaled was the leader of his people. A man familiar with the stories buried deep in the desert. And the pirates knew it. That's why they hadn't killed him. Not yet.

The pirate captain left his vessel in the hands of a small crew, while he and a band of his men were ferried to the shore, along with their prisoner.

Since then, they'd been travelling overland on a treacherous journey through the desert. Khaled's wrists were shackled, his clothes tattered, but his back remained ramrod straight and proud.

Captain Malik stood before him, his long red robes billowing, a sabre tucked into his belt and a cobra tattoo curling down his neck. His eyes were like glass – reflecting everything, revealing nothing.

'I tire of waiting, Khaled,' he snapped, tapping his foot impatiently. 'Tell us where to find the entrance to the hidden city.'

'I've already told you,' Khaled replied, his voice hoarse. 'No one alive knows where it is.'

Captain Malik smiled thinly. 'And yet your son carries the pearl that opens the gate. Do you expect me to believe he found it by chance?'

At the mention of Zayed's name, Khaled's jaw tightened. He wondered how the pirate knew about the pearl, but then remembered Malik carrying a telescope when he boarded the dhow.

'You leave my son out of this,' he said.

'Oh, I would,' Malik replied, circling him like a hawk, 'but the sand spirits say otherwise. They've seen a falcon circling over the old *wadi*. That means the boy lives... and he's close.'

He nodded to his first mate, a gaunt man with half his face burned away and eyes like dark coals.

‘Take him from my sight,’ said the captain. ‘Leave him without water for a while. The sun softens the stubborn.’

As the first mate dragged him away, the pirate leant closer, whispering into Khaled’s ear, the man’s foul, putrid breath making him gag.

‘You should talk,’ he whispered. ‘Give Malik what he wants. Not for your sake, but for your son’s.’

Then they left him alone. Khaled sat on the sand and closed his eyes.

He could still remember the stories his father had told him as a child. Tales of the “*city beneath the sand*”, where the ancients had sealed away a great power – its key, a pearl of perfect light, forged in sorrow and silence, A pearl that had been safely hidden far away, protected by the deep sea. A pearl meant never to be found.

But now it *had* been found... by Zayed.

A flicker of pain crossed Khaled’s face. He had never told his son everything – not to protect the treasure, but to protect the boy. The pearl drew attention from those of evil intent. From pirates. From djinn. From the Sandshadows. And something worse. Something Khaled had only seen once, long ago, when he was a boy... something buried beneath the city, older than time and hungry to be free.

As he thought about these things, things which he'd tried for so long to forget, he became aware of a faint sound. A whisper. Barely a breath. Khaled froze.

The shadows shifted. A shape formed, floating just above the ground – neither man nor beast – and almost transparent, like a phantom. Its voice slid into Khaled's mind like warmed oil. 'Your son is coming.'

Khaled didn't move. 'Leave him alone,' he said.

The shape swirled around him. 'But he brings the key.'

Khaled shook his head. 'I will never help you.'

The figure didn't speak again. It simply vanished into thin air, leaving behind a dark, damp patch on the sand where it had been.

Khaled bowed his head, heart pounding. He had to escape before Zayed reached the city. Before the gate opened. Before the thing beneath the sand woke again.

Khaled waited until the dead of night. Most of the pirates were asleep around the fires burning low on the sand. Only the quiet crackle of flames and the occasional grunt of a snoring man broke the silence.

Khaled had spent hours studying the shackles that bound him. Rusted and old – sloppy work. He'd seen better craftsmanship on water pots.

He waited until the single pirate left guarding him dozed off, slumped against a barrel with his head tilted back and his mouth wide open. Then Khaled moved.

From the hem of his tattered robe, he pulled out a thin sliver of bone, sharpened from the snapped rib of a goat they'd fed him days ago. It wasn't much, but he had patience... and calloused fingers from fishing for pearls. He slid the shard into the lock, tilting it gently, listening to the tiny clicks. One. Two. Almost there. A final twist, and then the lock popped. Khaled exhaled slowly.

Barefoot, he crept away from the camp, avoiding the sprawl of sleeping men and their outstretched limbs.

Freedom shimmered like a mirage in the distance. He was halfway to open ground when...

'Where do you think you're going?'

The voice stopped him cold.

Captain Malik stood behind him, arms folded, robes billowing. Around him, five pirates emerged from the shadows – silent, ready, as if they'd been expecting him all along.

Khaled didn't speak.

Malik took a step closer, unsheathing his curved blade. 'You disappoint me. What a pity! I thought you understood our agreement. You cooperate, you live. You run... and I start getting *creative*.'

'You won't find the city,' said Khaled. 'You think you know the way, but the desert doesn't yield to greed. Only to sacrifice.'

Malik smiled, but it didn't reach his eyes. 'Oh, I don't need the *desert* to yield. I just need *you* to.'

He gestured to the guards who surged forward, forcing Khaled down onto the ground. Two of them wrenched his arms behind his back, binding him again. The third held a knife far too close to his throat for comfort.

Malik stepped up and whispered, 'We've searched every dune from here to the Dry Teeth. And every time, the trail runs cold. But your tribe guards the last entrance. And you, Khaled, are the only one who can lead us in.'

Khaled's mouth set in a determined line. 'I won't betray them.'

'Oh, but you already have,' said Malik, producing a scroll from inside his robe.

The pirate captain unrolled it, revealing an old map inked on dried gazelle skin, etched with stars, strange markings, and a symbol Khaled knew only too well – an open eye, carved in sand – one of the marks of his tribe.

Malik tapped a spot just above it. 'Your son is walking this path now. The same one you took as a boy. The same one that leads to the city's threshold.'

Khaled's heart contracted.

'He carries the pearl, doesn't he?' Malik asked, his voice soft now. 'I know he has it. Don't lie to me. I can *smell* it on you. That magic, that ancient, humming power.'

Khaled said nothing. He didn't have to. This pirate seemed to know everything.

The captain smiled again. 'That pearl is the key. And your son will unlock the door for us.' He turned away. 'Chain him again. And double the guards.'

As they dragged Khaled away, he strained against his captors – not in anger, but in fear. Fear, not for himself, but for Zayed.

He had been wrong to keep so much from the boy. The hidden city was no treasure trove. It was a trap – a vault for an ancient evil sealed long ago, before time forgot its name. An evil that *wanted* to be found. That *needed* the pearl to wake. And now, Zayed was walking straight into its arms.

Chapter 13

The dunes were unlike any they'd seen before. They rolled in endless waves, high and smooth, glowing golden by day and silver under the stars. But it wasn't their size that unsettled the children – it was the sound. The wind didn't whistle or howl here. It whispered in endless, shifting voices riding on the breeze. Too faint to understand, but impossible to ignore.

Max's fur began to bristle the moment they arrived. 'I'm not imagining that, am I?' he asked. 'You can all hear those voices, right?'

Charlie glanced over his shoulder. 'Yeah. I keep thinking someone's calling my name.'

Zayed nodded. '*Hei* – yes. I remember the Whispering Dunes now, from some of the old stories. I think they guard the approach to the city.'

Jemima gripped the folds of her scarf tighter around her head. 'They guard them? How?'

But no one answered. They were all too on edge to speak now.

They moved carefully through the sand, following the path they'd seen etched on the watchtower map. The dunes shimmered, and shadows moved where no one stood. Even the falcon flew lower now, sticking close to them.

By mid-afternoon, the wind died altogether, and the dunes became strangely quiet. Even the desert had fallen silent.

'How much further?' asked Joe, his voice hoarse from the dry air.

'Not much,' replied Zayed, though his voice lacked the certainty it had earlier. 'But the closer we get, the more dangerous it will become.'

Jemima noticed that his gaze was constantly scanning the horizon, his posture tense as if expecting something – or someone – to appear at any moment. The desert had a way of playing tricks on the mind, and, as before, Jemima couldn't shake the feeling that they were being watched.

Later, as dusk began to fall, a sudden hoot pierced the stillness, cutting through the heavy silence like a sharp knife.

'What was that?' Joe asked, his eyes wide with surprise.

Zayed stopped in his tracks. 'An owl. But not just any owl.'

Jemima, Joe and Charlie exchanged confused glances.

'It's the desert owl,' Zayed said, his voice low and reverent. 'A creature of wisdom. It only appears when the desert has chosen its path. If the owl is here, I think we must be on the right track.'

Jemima's heart skipped a beat. 'You mean it's... guiding us, like the oryx did?'

Zayed nodded. 'Yes, but it's also a warning. The owl is said to be a guardian of the desert's secrets, much like the oryx. If it appears, it's a sign that we must tread carefully. The owl will only help those it deems worthy.'

Before they could say more, the owl appeared, its wings scything through the evening air like sharp blades. It flew low, gliding effortlessly over the ground, its round eyes glowing yellow in the moonlight. The owl was a striking figure, its feathers a deep, rich brown and white, with streaks of black across its chest. It was larger than any owl Jemima had ever seen, its wingspan wide and commanding.

The owl landed on a rock just ahead, its eyes fixed intently on them.

'Look,' Jemima said in a hushed voice. 'I think it's waiting for us.'

Zayed nodded. '*Hei* – yes, it will wait until we prove ourselves.'

The owl's yellow eyes seemed to pierce through the darkness, watching them carefully. Its hoot echoed again, softer this time, as if it were calling them forward.

'This is the way,' Zayed said, moving cautiously towards the owl. 'It wants us to follow.'

Jemima hesitated. 'But do we trust it?'

Zayed's eyes were full of resolve. 'Do we have a choice?'

They looked at Falak. He nodded.

The owl lifted its wings and took flight once more, swooping just over their heads, leading them further.

Falak followed in its slipstream, vigilant, eyes scanning the horizon.

As they reached the edge of a small ridge, they saw it – the crumbling ruins rising from the sand, like a forgotten memory of a time long past, jagged and sharp, with stone pillars and walls half-buried in the shifting sand. The cracked columns cast long, eerie shadows over the desolate landscape.

Jemima felt a shiver run down her spine. There was something otherworldly about the place, as if the town held secrets too old for human comprehension.

'So, if we've got this right,' said Zayed, 'the treasure is buried beneath these ruins. But my father said there are guardians who protect it – spirits from the past.'

'Oh, great, *more* spirits.' said Joe, forcing out a laugh to cover his nerves. 'Why am I not surprised? Oh well, I guess we should be used to spirits from the past by now. What harm can a few more do?'

The owl flew at a steady pace, gliding smoothly through the night air, its form almost disappearing into the shadows of the dunes.

They followed it through the winding ruins of the ancient town, passing shattered columns and crumbling walls that had once been part of a temple dedicated to long-forgotten gods. The owl's hoots guided them like a beacon, and although they were weary from the journey, Jemima couldn't help but feel a strange sense of purpose.

The further they went, the more the desert seemed to come alive around them. The wind whispered through the ruins, carrying with it the faint scent of something sweet, like jasmine or incense. But there was something else – something deeper, older – that resonated in the air, like the heartbeat of the desert itself.

Then, without warning, the owl stopped and perched on a stone altar, its wings folded tight against its body. It rotated its head to face them, its golden eyes glowing in the dark.

'The owl has led us here for a reason,' Zayed said quietly. 'What is it?'

Falak landed beside them. 'The Gate of Whispers lies just ahead,' he said.

Jemima shivered. They'd reached the main part of the temple where the air seemed thick with ancient power. In front of them stood a large arched doorway, half-covered by sand.

'There it is,' Zayed murmured, his voice filled with awe. 'Is this the way in?'

They stood before it in silence.

The arch seemed to be part of a larger structure, now swallowed by the desert. Most of it lay hidden beneath layers of time, but the magic still pulsed, steady and strange.

'If the entrance to the buried city is here,' Zayed continued, 'we need to open it somehow.'

'And how are we supposed to do that?' asked Joe.

Zayed looked at the owl, still watching them

with its piercing gaze. 'He knows the way, but we must prove our worth before he'll show us.'

To one side of the arch, a ring of flat, circular stones set one inside the other, sat like a sundial on a pedestal. Strange symbols and inscriptions covered its surface. They glowed faintly in the shifting light, dancing with the patterns in the sand.

When Jemima took a cautious step towards it, she noticed that the symbols on the stone seemed to shift slightly, as though responding to her presence. She reached out, her fingers brushing the surface.

The moment her skin made contact, the symbols flared to life, glowing faintly, casting a soft light on the sand around them. Jemima gasped, stepping back.

'What's happening?' she asked, stunned.

Max jumped down from Ghazala's back to stand beside Jemima, He ran a paw across the markings. 'These are instructions,' he said. 'It's some kind of test.'

Jemima turned to the cat, wondering how he knew that. 'What kind of test?'

Max squinted back at the markings. Something had stirred deep within him. He blinked, not understanding how that had popped into his head. But now he remembered what he'd had to do when he'd been in the underground tunnel before, when he'd had to open the gate that led to the garden where the lamp was. 'You have to answer,' he said. 'Not just with words, but with memory.'

Jemima stared at him. Yes, this was her cat speaking, but it didn't sound like him at all. His eyes were slightly glazed and his voice sounded as if it was reciting something that he'd been told to say. A shiver ran down her spine. 'I'm not sure what you mean, Max,' she said.

Zayed's eyebrows drew closer together. 'The desert is testing us,' he said, frowning. 'The symbols represent the ancient knowledge of this place, and they recognise us. But we must show that we're worthy by solving the puzzle.'

Jemima glanced at Charlie, who was already deep in concentration as he studied the strange markings. He was good at solving puzzles.

The owl watched them silently with its unblinking yellow eyes.

'This doesn't make sense,' Charlie murmured. 'The symbols are like a riddle, but there's something missing. A piece of the puzzle.'

Zayed shook his head. 'We have to think like the ancients. The desert itself is the key. The sand, the wind, the stars. They all have their place in this puzzle.'

Charlie looked up at the sky, his mind working overtime. The stars twinkled overhead, scattered across the vast expanse of midnight velvet like diamonds. He thought of the desert's magic – the same magic that had brought them here, that had guided them to the ruins. The symbols on the door seemed to glimmer in time with the stars, as if they were connected somehow.

Suddenly, he had an idea. He turned to the owl. 'The stars,' he said softly. 'We need to align the symbols with the stars, don't we?'

The owl gave a low hoot of approval. Its wings fluttered slightly, as if urging him to continue.

Charlie turned back to the stone dials and took a step closer, placing his hand on the one closest to him. The stone felt alive, vibrating with energy. Slowly, carefully, he rotated the outer ring, aligning the symbols with the positions of the stars above... but still nothing happened.

Falak swooped down, landing beside the door. 'This city was never meant to be found by the greedy. Only those who carry *truth* are permitted to enter, only those who are pure of heart. You must prove who you are before you're allowed inside.' The falcon turned to Zayed. 'Take out the pearl.'

Zayed removed the pearl from his bag. At once, the arch began to hum, and the symbols glowed brighter. The sand around them shifted.

With a deep rumble, the door began to move, the sand that had buried it for centuries sliding away as it creaked open. A faint light leaked from within, casting eerie shadows across the desert floor.

'Hey, we did it,' Joe whispered. 'Look, it's opening. Let's go in.'

But before they could do anything, they heard raucous shouts carried on the wind. The pirates were close. The children knew they must enter the underground city before their pursuers got there.

Chapter 14

The open gap revealed a second arch inside, twice as wide as the first, and lined with statues worn smooth by time. The air turned cool, like stepping into shade after hours in the sun. The ground trembled.

And then the whispers grew louder, the words became clearer.

'Zayed, child of the *Ra'is*, why do you seek what was buried?'

Zayed's eyes widened. It knew his name and that his father was the *chief* of their tribe. His mouth opened, but no sound came out.

'You have to answer with what you feel – the truth,' whispered Max. 'Don't lie. Don't hide it.'

Zayed took a breath. 'For my father, Khaled,' he said. 'Because he was taken by pirates. Because he's in danger. Because this city may be the only way to save him. I don't know...'

The wind picked up, growing stronger, brushing their cheeks like invisible fingers.

The whisper continued. 'And if saving him means waking what sleeps beneath?'

Zayed faltered. He didn't know what that meant. What was he supposed to say?

Seeing Zayed struggle to answer the question, Charlie stepped forward. 'Then we'll stop it, whatever it is – together.'

At once, the gate opened with a groan. A massive stone slid aside, revealing a dark passageway descending into the earth. Cool air gusted out, smelling of age and long forgotten scents... and something else they couldn't identify, but it wasn't pleasant – an odour of rot and decay.

Max stood rooted to the spot. He hadn't seen any of this the last time. The part of the underground city he'd been in before was totally different – tunnels and chambers, accessed by a hidden trapdoor beside the dunes.

'Come on, let's move,' said Joe, gripping the strap of his water skin tighter. 'Before the pirates get here.'

'Do you think it's safe to go down there?' asked Jemima, sounding apprehensive. 'I mean, the door just opened on its own. What if it decides to shut again, trapping us inside?'

Zayed was silent for a moment, his gaze

fixed on the dark corridor ahead of them. 'We're here now, so I guess we have to take the risk. We don't have much choice.'

'Okay, let's go,' said Joe, trying to steady his nerves.

'Even Ghazala?' asked Jemima.

'All of us,' said Falak. 'We must stick together.'

'Okay, but I hope there's enough room for her down there,' said Joe. He moved forward, his footsteps muffled by the thick layer of dust that covered the ground.

The others followed him, the sound of their breathing echoing in the stillness.

They came to a vast circular chamber. Three tunnels led off in different directions. An image was carved on the wall beside the entrance to each one – a flame, an eye and a coiled serpent.

'Which way do we go?' asked Jemima.

'Don't choose the snake,' pleaded Max.

'We'll try the flame,' said Zayed. 'Maybe that will lead us to the lamp.'

The further they walked, the colder the air became. The stone walls of the passageway narrowed, forcing them to move in single file. It was a tight squeeze for Ghazala.

The faint scent of ancient wood and decay filled the air. But the deeper they went, the more oppressive the silence became – like the weight of centuries pressing in on them.

At the end of the passage, they found a large chamber. The walls were lined with faded frescoes, their once-vibrant colours now worn away by time. The room was vast, its ceiling lost in the shadows above. And on the ground, spread among the stones, were the remains of the long-dead.

Jemima's breath caught in her throat. The skeletons lay scattered across the floor, their bones picked clean by time and scavengers. Some were in sitting positions, others were lying in twisted heaps, their limbs splayed unnaturally, as if they had died in terror.

There were dozens of them, all lying in various poses, some half-buried beneath layers of dust and sand. Their skulls stared up at the ceiling, empty eye sockets dark and hollow.

'Blimey, this is horrible,' whispered Charlie. 'What happened to them? Why are they here?'

Zayed's face was grim. 'These were the people who came seeking the treasure – the ones who never returned. The desert claimed them, just as it will claim us if we're not careful.'

Jemima swallowed hard. 'But... why? What happened to them?'

Zayed pointed to the wall, where the carvings had been partially preserved. The images depicted people, dressed in ancient robes, kneeling before a large hoard of glittering treasure, the chests overflowing with gold coins and jewels. But the figures in the carvings had solemn expressions, as if they knew something terrible was about to happen.

'The treasure,' Zayed said quietly, his voice heavy with foreboding. 'It's cursed. The people who sought it were warned. Remember the oryx, the owl... they are the guardians of this place. So, these people knew that the treasure wasn't meant to be found. But they ignored the warnings and they came anyway.'

Charlie's heart pounded in his chest. 'So, they... they died because they tried to take the treasure?'

Zayed nodded grimly. '*Hei* – yes. The desert does not forgive those who try to steal from it. The bones you see here are the remains of those who thought they could conquer the desert's secrets. But the desert takes what it wants. And the treasure... it isn't just gold. I think there's something much older and darker buried beneath this city.'

Jemima shivered. 'I don't like this. We need to go back. This whole place is cursed.' She reached for Joe's arm.

'We can't leave now,' said Zayed, determination hardening his expression. 'Not without the answers. We must go on.'

Jemima nodded, despite the unease coiling in her stomach. 'Okay, but we have to be careful, especially if the treasure is more than just gold – if it's something else, something dangerous.'

She glanced at Charlie, both of them reluctant to head further into the dark chamber of death. But Zayed's resolve was unshakable. Nothing was going to change his mind now.

Perched silently on a block of stone, Falak watched them as they made their decision to continue. Then, with a click of his beak, he unfolded his wings and took flight, beckoning to them to follow.

They moved forward cautiously, stepping over the bones that littered the chamber. Falak led the way, his wings slicing through the air as he navigated the ancient ruins with ease. But every step felt heavier, as if the desert itself was holding its breath, waiting for something to happen.

The deeper they went into the labyrinth of ancient chambers, the more oppressive the atmosphere became. The walls seemed to close in, the shadows thickening as if something was watching them. The ancient skeletons, the cursed treasure, and the desert's watchful guardians – they were all part of something much larger than they could have imagined.

With nerves jangling, they went through the gate. As they descended into the darkness, torches magically flickered to life along the walls. The stairs led deeper, turning into smooth corridors lined with ancient carvings and relics that spoke of a forgotten civilisation that once ruled the desert, of a great treasure hidden far below. The walls were covered in paintings depicting a once-great city, its towers rising, its streets filled with people, its light powered by a pearl on top of a glowing lamp.

In the centre of it all sat a figure with no face, arms outstretched, sealed behind a wall of flame.

Jemima stared. 'What on earth is *that*?'

Falak's eyes gleamed in the torchlight. 'That,' he said softly, 'is what the pearl was meant to keep from waking up. Don't look at it and certainly don't go any nearer. Back away – *shway,*

shway – slowly. Don't give in to it. Stay strong.'

'But what *is* it?' said Joe, taking a step towards it to get a closer look.

'You don't need to know, other than it's pure evil and it must never be allowed to escape,' explained the falcon. 'If it was ever released into the world, it would wreak untold havoc, destruction and disaster. You must keep right away. So, do as I say and move back. NOW!'

Jemima shuddered, sensing an aura of something malevolent desperate to escape from its prison. She felt it trying to reel them in, drawing them towards it with a powerful force.

'Let's keep going,' urged Zayed with a shudder. It took all his strength to resist the magnetic pull of its outstretched arms.

Leaving the writhing, evil figure behind, they turned away, moving deeper into the forgotten city. The further they went, they began to feel the ancient forces waiting beneath the sand.

Above them, far across the Whispering Dunes, the wind was rising again. A loud, chilling cry echoed through the desert. The pirates were coming. The children knew there would be no escape from them unless they unlocked the mysteries of the buried city... and fast.

Chapter 15

Captain Malik stood at the edge of the Whispering Dunes, the wind tugging at his crimson robe, his sabre gleaming. Behind him, the pirates readied themselves – a dozen men, armed to the teeth, their weathered faces grim.

Before them, the dunes rippled like a golden sea. A vast silence stretched over the land... until the whispers began.

'Is that the wind?' asked one of the crew, glancing nervously over his shoulder.

'It's not wind,' said the First Mate, eyes narrowed. 'That sounds more like voices.'

Malik smiled thinly. 'Good. That means we're close.'

He stepped forward and the sand beneath his boots seemed to shift unnaturally, as if protesting his presence. The further they marched, the louder the whispers grew. The air pressed down on them like invisible hands. A few of the men faltered.

'This place is cursed,' said one. 'We shouldn't be here.'

Malik spun around to glare at him, his voice sharp. 'You think a few whispers will scare *me*? We've sailed through storms, fought battles and sea monsters. This,' he gestured to the dunes, 'is just sand.'

But the dunes didn't agree.

As the pirates continued, one of the crew suddenly sank up to his knees in fine dust. He screamed and struggled as the sand pulled harder. Two others ran to help, grabbing his arms. They yanked as hard as they could, but only his tunic came free. The man was gone.

'Move!' barked Malik. 'Do as I say. Stay light, stay fast. Step only where I step.'

Spooked by what had just happened, they proceeded more carefully now. The shadows grew longer. The whispers began to change – no longer just sounds, but words and names.

'Thieves.'

'Raiders.'

'Pirates.'

'Malik.'

The First Mate turned to the captain, his eyes wide in fear. 'They know your name, boss.'

'Ha! They'll certainly remember my name after *this*,' Malik replied coldly. 'Once we take the city's riches, I'll be famous throughout history.'

They crested a dune just as the last sunbeam struck the horizon. Below them lay the faint remains of a stone arch – mostly buried – the entrance to a place none of them had ever seen before, but all of them somehow felt as if they recognised it.

The Gate of Whispers.

'Look, it's open,' said the First Mate. He pointed to the shifting sand at its base. 'They got here before us. They're already inside.'

Malik's eyes gleamed. 'Good! Then we follow. They've done the work for us.'

Behind him, the pirates descended towards the gate. The ground groaned beneath their feet. Whispers rose to screams – not of pain, but of warning.

And the wind carried a single phrase, repeated again and again: 'Do not wake what sleeps below.'

But Malik didn't flinch. He drew his sabre, his voice low and certain. 'Too late,' he said.

Chapter 16

The children moved through the tunnel in single file, their footsteps echoing softly against ancient stone. The air was cool and dry, laced with the scent of dust and ancient incense from a distant past. Strange symbols lit up along the walls as they passed – pale blue motifs that quivered gently, as though the city itself had stirred from sleep.

They passed statues of tall, robed figures with eyes like stars, holding aloft lamps that seemed to shine in stone. At their feet were coils – snakes, shadows, things without names.

'They weren't just builders,' Max whispered, perched on Jemima's shoulder. 'They were guardians.'

'Guardians of what?' she asked, keeping close to Zayed. 'Was it the Guardians of Time?'

'No, I think they were the Guardians of the Pearl,' Zayed said softly. 'And also of the evil thing it was keeping locked up, like Falak told us.'

Jemima stopped beside a large mural, one

hand brushing over the carved surface. In the centre was a blazing lamp, encircled by a colossal figure forged of scorched air and curling smoke, wrapped around a skeletal frame. Iron chains held the monstrous creature captive, their links threading around the whole city like roots of despair.

'Is *that* it?' she said. 'It looks trapped.'

Falak fluttered onto a broken column. 'That's because it *is* trapped. The evil was sealed beneath the city long ago. The pearl is the key to its prison... and the lamp is the lock.'

A hush fell over them, as they tried to make sense of this.

Then, from deep within the passage ahead, a distant grinding sound echoed – the sound of stone on stone. A door was opening.

Max's ears pricked up, hearing a noise from behind them. 'We're not alone anymore,' he whispered.

******

Far above, Captain Malik stepped through the open gate. The pirates followed cautiously, weapons drawn. The air shifted around them, thick with ancient magic. As they moved through the tunnel, they passed the same glowing motifs... but in their presence, the light turned dull and red.

'Even the walls don't like us,' muttered one crewman.

Malik said nothing. His eyes were locked ahead.

At the first chamber – a vast circular room with three branching tunnels – he paused.

'Which way do we go?' asked the First Mate.

The captain turned towards the wall, where a massive stone map was carved into the surface. The image of a pearl marked the centre. Three lines radiated out, each leading to a separate chamber – one marked with a flame, one with an eye, and one with a coiled serpent.

'We split up,' said Malik. 'Three teams. We search them all. Find the pearl. Find the lamp.'

The men grumbled but obeyed. As they disappeared into the tunnels, the Gate of Whispers sealed shut behind them with a deep, echoing *boom*.

The city had accepted them... but it had not welcomed them.

******

Deeper still, the children had entered a long gallery lit by shafts of amber light filtering from vents in the ceiling. The murals here were different – less majestic, more desperate. One showed robed figures fleeing in terror. Another showed the pearl cracked in two, and shadows pouring from the wound.

Charlie shivered. 'I think something might have escaped from here,' he said.

Zayed touched the carving. 'Or it *almost* did, but something else stopped it. Do you think it was the lamp?'

Falak tilted his head. '*Hei* – Yes, and you must find it before the pirates do, or everything this city protected will fall.'

They kept going, hearts racing.

******

In another corridor, one of the pirate scouts stepped too close to a cracked tile on the ground.

They all heard a sudden *hiss* as a dozen needle-thin darts fired from the wall. He dropped without a sound.

The others backed away quickly.

'There are hidden traps,' cried the First

Mate, his eyes widening in horror. 'And they're still active.'

But Malik only smiled. 'Good. That means no one else has been here in centuries.'

He turned to a nearby alcove, where a strange shape sat upon a stone pedestal – gleaming in gold, with a long spout, and wrapped in silvery wire. A lamp.

But it was only a copy – a decoy to trick unwary raiders.

Taking a deep breath, Malik took a step towards it and reached out, but wasn't fooled. He quickly withdrew his hand when he saw it wasn't the real thing. 'We're getting close,' he said.

******

Far below, the children reached a sealed door, circular and decorated with pearl inlay that shimmered faintly as Zayed approached. He took the pearl from his bag and raised his hand.

The door vibrated in response, then slid open with a breath of cool air. Inside was a spiral staircase, descending into darkness.

Joe looked at the others. 'I guess there's no turning back now.'

They stepped inside.

As the door shut behind them, they heard a whisper rise from the walls.

'The key has returned. The seal grows weak,' it said.

And somewhere below, in a chamber of dust and broken chains, something stirred. It writhed and slithered, then opened its eyes.

Chapter 17

The staircase spiralled down and down, winding deep into the belly of the earth. Stone gave way to smooth walls of polished quartz, veined with shimmering gold and etched with thousands of tiny carvings. The deeper they went, the quieter everything became until even the sound of their breathing felt too loud. Finally, the stairs opened into a vast hall, half-lit by a soft, golden glow that came from the walls themselves.

It was a place lost to time. More statues lined the chamber – tall, hooded figures with outstretched hands, each holding a relic – an hourglass of stone, a key, an owl, and a book with pages of hammered gold.

On the walls behind them, the carvings told the story of a civilisation older than the dunes. A people who commanded light and shadow. Builders of oases and guardians of the stars. At the height of their power, they created the pearl – not as a treasure, but as a key to a prison.

Something bad had come from beneath the world, from the dark between sand and sky, and they had locked it away.

In the centre of the hall, a low stone platform rose from the ground. Carved into it was the shape of the city itself, with pathways that curled inward like a spiral maze.

'It's a map,' said Jemima, eyes wide.

Charlie moved closer, studying the details. 'It looks like it shows every chamber. But d'you see those markings? I think they could be traps. And this one, here, might be a puzzle.'

Max hopped onto the platform and stared. He tilted his head. 'I think I've seen something like this before.'

'Oh, here we go again,' said Joe. 'The magician conveniently left a copy of it for you to look at, did he?'

'Oh, shut up, Joe,' everybody chorused.

Joe was so surprised that his mouth snapped shut and he fell silent.

'Go on, Max. Tell us what you saw,' urged Zayed. 'Where was it?

'In an underground chamber,' murmured the cat, 'when I first came to this place. I was in a tunnel and I remember seeing a plan like this on one of the walls, but I didn't know what it was back then. I didn't take much notice of it, because I'd been given precise instructions that I had to follow. I was told to go past the three chambers with treasure in them and to head straight for a gate that led into a garden, because that was where I'd find the lamp. I realise now that there was probably much more that I didn't explore, but I wasn't keen to look around – I just wanted to get out of there.'

'So, how did you get out?' asked Zayed.

'When I escaped, it was through a cave on the other side of the garden. It led straight out into the desert. I didn't know there were any other gateways.' The cat tried to cast his mind back to the scene below ground once his eyes had become accustomed to the darkness. His tail twitched as a forgotten detail suddenly popped into his mind.

'Wait, I've just remembered something. 'When I came down the tunnel, there was a rhyme written on the wall – a riddle. I didn't think it was relevant, so didn't pay any attention to it.'

'What did it say?' asked Jemima.

Max closed his eyes, picturing the words. 'Left where water used to run, follow fire until it's done. Step where light and shadow meet or lose your soul beneath your feet.'

'Well, that sounds cheerful!' said Joe.

Max ignored him. 'If we're in a kind of maze, this could be a guide to show the way through it.'

'Yes, I think you could be right, Max,' said Charlie, patting the cat on the head. 'I don't quite understand what it all means, but it's telling us what we have to do.'

Zayed pointed to the spiral. 'Then that's where we go – the middle chamber. Look! It's marked with the symbol of a pearl.'

Falak fluttered up to a high perch, looking down at the plan from above. 'That must be where the lamp sleeps. If it still burns.'

Max wrinkled his snout. That didn't sound right to him. Why wasn't the lamp in the garden, like when he was there before?

Jemima took a deep breath. 'Okay, I guess we should head in there. You'd better lead the way, Max. This place might remember you from before and will know you're on the side of the good guys.'

They entered the first tunnel from the map. Almost immediately they heard a rumble. The floor trembled beneath their feet... and a row of tiles dropped away into darkness.

Max skidded to a halt with a sharp intake of breath. 'No one move.' He stared at the tiles, repeating, *'Light and shadow... light and shadow...'*

Then he saw it – faint lines etched into the stone above the pit. The shafts of light from the ceiling formed a pattern across the tiles – two safe ones in shadow, one lit. It was a trap.

'Only step on the ones that are half-lit,' he said, reciting the words from the rhyme. '*Where the light and dark cross.*'

Following his instructions, they moved one by one, carefully hopping across the tiles. Ghazala grunted nervously but obeyed. It wasn't easy for an animal of her size, especially with her big, wide feet. Falak flew safely above their heads.

Beyond the pit trap, the tunnel twisted into a hexagonal room with high ceilings and six doors. In the centre was a massive sundial, but there was no sun to illuminate its markings. It began to turn slowly as they entered, and all the doors glimmered with a strange light.

'Now, this is a time puzzle,' Max said at once. He had no idea how he seemed to know these things – he just did. 'The rhyme said, "*Left where water used to run...*" Hmm!'

He looked up at the stone lintel above one of the doors. It was carved with wavy lines and fish.

'It's this one. Go through it and turn left.'

They rushed towards it and all made it through just as the sundial groaned and the door slammed shut behind them.

The next chamber was worse. Once again, yet more statues lined the walls, but their faces were cracked and twisted. In the middle sat a pedestal which held a bowl of shimmering sand. Four stone hands reached for it, frozen in mid-air.

'Stand still,' whispered Charlie. 'I think there might be some kind of pressure plates here.'

'What are pressure plates?' asked Zayed.

'Well, if you pick up the bowl, for example, you might trigger one, and then something happens,' he explained. 'Maybe a hole in the floor opens up and you fall through it?'

Joe peered at the floor. 'Cool! This is like something from *Raiders of the Lost Ark*.'

'Raiders of the Lost *what*?' said Zayed with a puzzled frown.

'You know... Indiana Jones,' replied Joe. 'All I need is one of those hats and a whip.'

This confused Zayed even more. 'Why? What do you need a whip for? You're strange.'

'Of course he doesn't know who Indiana Jones is, Joe,' Jemima said, shaking her head. Her brother was such a noodle at times. She turned to Zayed. 'Um, it's just a story... where we come from.'

'Ah, perhaps like the *Tales of One Thousand and One Nights*?' suggested Falak.

'Yes, something like that... maybe,' said Charlie, remembering that *The Thousand and One Nights*, or *The Arabian Nights*, contained the story of the *Magic Lamp*.

'Well, whatever,' said Joe, still staring at the floor. 'So, how do we reach the bowl?'

'We don't,' said Max. 'We leave it. Watch out, because I think the sand could be a trap as well. Don't touch anything.' His whiskers twitched.

Jemima's eyes widened at Max's amazing knowledge about these mystical things. How had he got so clever all of a sudden? She didn't realise it was all part of the magic and the powers bestowed on him by the Guardians of Time. Even Max, himself, didn't realise this.

They moved through the next corridor, and slowly, the temperature dropped. The carvings on the walls showed flames, storms, and a dark shadowy figure rising upwards. Then, finally, ahead of them, they saw it.

A chamber filled with pillars of glass and gold, ancient and cracked. In the middle, on top of a square block of obsidian, burned a single blue flame, its light reflecting in the glossy black stone.

Was this the lamp?

It glimmered with the same soft light as the pearl. As they stepped closer, the flame flickered as if it recognised them.

Jemima reached out slowly. 'Is this *it*, Max? Have we found it?'

And as they all turned towards the lamp, the carvings on the walls seemed to shimmer, the eyes of the statues glowing faintly.

The city was opening its heart.

But just then, behind them, far down the tunnels, a low, distant *clang* echoed through the halls.

'I think someone's just triggered one of the traps,' said Charlie.

'The pirates are getting closer,' Zayed murmured. 'We only have a few moments.'

Max's fur suddenly stood up in stiff spikes. 'Something's wrong,' he whispered. 'The lamp knows they're almost here.'

And then, the most extraordinary thing happened. Just as Zayed reached out to pluck the lamp from the block of jet-black stone, a dazzling flash of light filled the chamber. They blinked and when they looked again the lamp was gone, vanished right before their very eyes. In its place lay a small branch with a golden leaf and a perfect white bloom.

'Wha...?' Joe's mouth dropped open in surprise. 'Where did it go?'

'I think I know,' said Max, seeing the white flower and the leaf. 'The tree, in the garden...'

As he spoke, they heard another grinding noise and a door they hadn't spotted before slowly began to swing open.

'Are we meant to go through there?' asked Zayed.

'Yes, I think so,' said Max, suddenly sure that this was the right thing to do. He glanced at the falcon who nodded his approval.

'Let's hurry, then,' said Zayed. 'Before the pirates come this way.'

As they stepped through the doorway, they found themselves in another tunnel, with a trail of white petals leading off into the darkness.

'Why are there no lights through here?' asked Jemima, her fingers fumbling along the rough stone walls as she tried to feel her way.

'Because this is a passageway no one was supposed to find,' said Falak.

'But I recognise it,' said Max, feeling excitement bubbling up inside him. 'This is the place I know – the same tunnel I was in the last time I was here.' He looked up. Far above their heads, he could just make out a faint glimmer of light around the edges of a trapdoor. 'See, that's where the magician lowered me down from.'

'I can't see a thing,' said Joe. 'It's pitch-black in here.'

'Too bad,' said Max, sounding smug. 'But I'm a cat and *I* can see in the dark.'

'Take out the pearl, Zayed,' said the falcon.

Zayed slipped the pearl from his bag and held it on the palm of his hand. Its faint pink glow was just enough for them to be able to see one another. Although the tunnel with its rough walls lay in deep shadow, they no longer felt blinded by the darkness.

'Look,' said Max. 'There's the carving of the maze on the wall that I told you about – just like I remembered.' He arched his brow as he stared at Joe. 'And it looks like the one we just saw.'

Joe's gaze slid sideways. He hated to admit it, but Max had been right.

'There's the rhyme too – the riddle,' said Jemima.

Zayed read it out loud. *'Left where water used to run, follow fire until it's done. Step where light and shadow meet or lose your soul beneath your feet.* Are there traps down here too?'

'I don't remember any,' said Max. 'But we should be careful, just in case.'

'So, we turn left down here?' asked Charlie.

'Yes,' said the large cat, his confidence fully returned. He set off down the passageway. 'I know the way now. Follow me.' It was just as he remembered from before.

They all hurried to keep up with him as he made his way down the tunnel until he reached a door at the far end.

'Once we go through here,' explained the cat, 'it's important that you follow my instructions. We will pass three arches. Whatever you do, you must not set foot in any of those chambers, however tempting they might appear. They're filled with treasure. Do you understand?'

They all nodded, as Max stood in front of the doorway.

He took a deep breath, trying to remember the exact words he'd used before.

'I am Maximus, the son of Merlin and Sabrina,' he chanted in a loud, clear voice.

A ghostly echo repeated the phrase. Hearing it bounce off the walls, Jemima jumped. The voice didn't sound like Max at all.

They held their breath, waiting to see what would happen next. All was silent for a moment and then, the door began to creak slowly inwards.

Max hesitated for a second before stepping into the corridor beyond, with the others right behind him. Just as he'd described, they saw an open archway on their left. When they peered inside, none of them were able to contain their gasps of wonder at the sight of treasure chests overflowing with rivers of glistening gold whose buttery glow illuminated the entire chamber.

'You mustn't step over the threshold,' Max reminded them.

The second doorway revealed coffers filled with silver, running over the sides in shimmering streams that lit up the gloom, but the best was still to come.

The third chamber was heaped with mounds of precious gemstones – sparkling with the fire of diamonds, rubies and sapphires, all nestled amongst clusters of creamy pearls.

'No wonder the pirates want to get their hands on all of this,' said Joe. He took a step towards the entrance, but a sudden screech from Falak stopped him in his tracks.

Max glared at him. 'I said no, Joe.'

'I just wanted a closer look,' Joe replied with a huff. 'There's no need to be so bossy.'

'There's every need, young man,' said the falcon clicking his beak crossly. 'You must do as Max says. He knows best.'

Scowling, Joe bit back the retort that was on the tip of his tongue.

'See the gate at the end?' Max said breathlessly. 'That's it – the entrance into the garden.'

As if by magic, the wrought iron grille swung open as they approached.

With a sigh of relief, Max stepped through it and found himself in the beautiful underground garden that he remembered from before. He'd done it.

Entranced, they gazed around, scarcely able to believe what they were seeing. Bathed in a pale, silvery glow, it was a slice of paradise deep below the earth, filled with light and shadow.

'Wow,' murmured Jemima, noting the lush vegetation and the myriad of scented, colourful flowers.

Joe gasped, before turning to Max with a sheepish expression. 'It's real! But how is this even possible? I didn't believe you.'

'I know,' replied the cat, flattening his ears.

'Where's the lamp?' Zayed asked. 'I know this is lovely, but we don't have time to stand around admiring the view. Every minute that passes brings the pirates a step closer.'

Max nodded his head towards the large tree standing in the middle of the garden, its boughs laden with creamy, fragrant blossom. 'Over there,' he said.

They walked all around the tree, gazing up through its dense foliage. Then they saw it. Perched on a branch high above their heads, sat the golden lamp. It had moved itself to a place of safety when it had heard the pirates approach, but now it was almost within their grasp once more.

'How do we get it down?' asked Jemima.

'Easy,' said Zayed, used to shinning up palm trees in search of dates. He jumped onto one of the branches that hung low to the ground and in no time had climbed up high enough to stretch out his hand to reach the lamp.

'Careful,' Jemima cried. 'Don't drop it.'

'I won't.' With a firm grip on the handle,

Zayed swung his way back down to the ground and passed it to her. 'Here, take it from me,' he said.

The lamp hummed in Jemima's hands. Even unlit, it gave off a warmth that she could feel right through to her bones – strange, comforting, alive.

'What do we do next?' she asked.

'Can you kneel down so I can reach it?' said Max.

Doing as he asked, Jemima held the lamp out towards him.

'This is what I did before.' With a large, velvety grey paw, the cat gently rubbed the shiny golden surface.

At first, only a small blue flame danced gently from its spout but then, a sudden dazzling flash of bright light, accompanied by a loud bang, made them almost jump out of their skins. When the smoke cleared, even Joe gaped at the sight of the towering figure hovering before their eyes.

The genie fixed its gaze on Max. '*As-salaam alaikum* – Greetings! You have released me from the lamp once again, Master, and I am here to serve you. What is your desire?'

'*Marhaba* – Hello,' said Max with a polite nod. 'Please wait a moment.' The cat turned to the children. 'What should we ask for?'

'We must use his help to save Zayed's father,' said Jemima.

'And also to protect my tribe,' said Zayed.

'But we need to make sure the pirates never find the lamp,' added Charlie.

'Please remember that you have but a *single* wish,' said the genie, bowing his head. 'Use the power wisely, for it can be both a blessing and a curse.'

'Do we have to decide right now?' Jemima asked. 'Maybe we should hold off using the wish to be sure we make the right choice?'

They all agreed this was the most sensible thing to do, so Max placed a paw on the lamp and looked the genie in the eye. 'I agree with Jemima,' he said. 'We will wait until the time is right.'

'As you wish, Master,' replied the genie. 'I will await your command.' With another flash of light, he disappeared in a puff of smoke.

Chapter 18

They retraced their steps, heading back the way they'd come. When they reached the chamber where they'd first seen the lamp, a thunderous *crack* suddenly rang out behind them – and then came the shouting. Boots on stone. Steel drawn. A red flare tossed into the chamber. The danger they'd feared had come at last. The pirates had caught up with them.

Jemima hastily wrapped the lamp in her scarf and held it out of sight behind her back.

'Run!' shouted Charlie.

They scattered as the pirates stormed into the chamber, their swords gleaming in the lamp's gentle glow. Captain Malik led the charge, his eyes locked on Zayed.

The boy's face turned pale at the sight of the pirates, their faces wrapped in black scarves, their eyes sharp with greed. Zayed recognised their leader, the man with the crooked nose and the cobra tattoo.

Captain Malik sneered at him from behind his mask. 'We've been looking for you, boy, and it seems we've found you at last,' he growled. 'You're coming with us. Your father will tell us the location of the treasure now, whether he wants to or not.'

Joe's heart thudded in his chest. The pirates had found them sooner than they'd expected, and now they were surrounded.

'We'll take the boy to our camp and make sure he tells us everything he knows. If anyone tries to follow us, they *won't* live to regret it.' Captain Malik's cold laughter echoed around the chamber.

Zayed tried to fight – ducking, twisting, slamming his shoulder into one of the pirates – but there were too many of them. One grabbed him from behind, yanking his arms back.

'Leave me. Run!' he shouted to the others. 'Get out of here.'

'No, Zayed!' Joe lunged forward, but Charlie pulled him back just in time as more pirates swarmed in.

Max hissed and launched himself at a pirate's face, scratching wildly before leaping away. 'There are too many of them,' yelled the cat. 'Get to the tunnels!'

Ghazala let out a war-cry of a snort, knocked

over two pirates with a swipe of her head, and bolted for the nearest archway with the others clinging to her back. They galloped out of the chamber as the pirates dragged Zayed in the opposite direction, Malik's cruel laughter echoing behind them.

'And I'll get the lamp,' the captain shouted, with a cackle. 'You can be sure of that.'

They didn't stop running until they reached the surface where dusk was now falling, streaking the desert with long orange shadows, but the pirates were nowhere to be seen. They'd gone... and they'd taken Zayed with them.

Falak circled above, his sharp eyes scanning the dunes.

'We have to find Zayed,' Jemima panted. 'They'll hurt him.'

'They won't,' said Max. 'Not yet. They need him.'

'Because they want the lamp,' Charlie said grimly. 'They'll trade him for it.'

Jemima looked down at the lamp glowing in her hands. 'Then we need to outsmart them. They're not getting their thieving mitts on this.'

******

At the pirates' camp, Zayed sat against a crumbling wall, wrists bound, face bruised, but eyes defiant. A short distance away, his father, Khaled, knelt with his arms tied behind his back.

'I'm sorry, Baba,' Zayed said quietly. 'I failed.'

'You have nothing to be sorry for, my son. And you did not fail,' murmured Khaled. 'You came further on your own than I ever hoped. Goodness knows how you found your way, but you managed it. You've done very well, and I'm so proud of you.'

Zayed hung his head in bitter regret. 'But it was all for nothing. He's got the pearl.'

Captain Malik stood by the fire, holding the pearl up to the dying light. 'And what a thing of beauty it is,' he murmured, lifting it higher to admire its rosy perfection. 'A priceless treasure in itself, but with this and the lamp together... imagine what doors I'll be able to open. And I will have them both... very soon.'

Just then, a shadow passed overhead.

Suddenly, Falak dived from the sky in a flash of wings and talons, snatching the pearl straight from the captain's fingers.

'No!' Malik shouted in fury, drawing his blade.

But the falcon was already gone, vanishing into the sky like a shadow chased by flame.

Only Zayed understood what had just happened. He'd recognised Falak at once and could barely stop himself from laughing out loud at the agonised look on the captain's face.

******

Falak let out a cry to announce his arrival and swooped down, landing on a boulder beside Max and the children.

'I saw where they went, so I followed,' the falcon said. 'An old ruin to the north - broken towers and a sunken courtyard. They've set up camp there.'

'Do they have Zayed's father as well?' asked Jemima.

Falak nodded. '*Hei* – yes. He's alive. But they took the pearl from Zayed. Their leader was holding it up to admire it when I struck.'

'You did *what?*' said Max, his ears twitching as he stared at the falcon.

Falak looked rather pleased with himself. 'I snatched the pearl from him and hid it somewhere safe. Come with me to fetch it and then let's go to their camp.'

'What for? We're no match for a band of pirates,' Charlie said disconsolately.

'Ah, but I have a plan,' said Falak, clicking his beak. 'Climb onto Ghazala's back. We'll rescue them – both of them – Zayed *and* his father.'

******

Panic rippled through the pirate camp after the bird of prey had swooped down and stolen the pearl. As the captain raged, his men yelled and scrambled to mount their horses, swords at the ready. And then came the thunder of feet pounding across the sand as Ghazala burst from the dunes, carrying Jemima, Joe, Charlie, and Max on her back. In Jemima's hand, the lamp flared with light.

'Let them go, or we'll turn the magic of the lamp on you,' she shouted. 'You'll regret it.'

Malik froze. Even he didn't know what powers the lamp could really unleash. He couldn't risk it.

'Do it, Jemima,' whispered Max. 'The lamp won't hurt *us*.'

Jemima raised the lamp high, and its blue flame suddenly roared into life, sending a wave of heat and light across the camp.

The sand lit up as if the sun had risen

beneath it. Winds blasted from nowhere, spinning a protective circle of dust around the children. The pirates staggered back, shielding their eyes.

Strange figures which looked as if they were made of glass rose from the sand, just for a moment – guardians summoned by the flame.

'Now!' Charlie shouted.

Falak swooped low, untangling Zayed's ropes with his talons and beak, while Joe and Charlie raced to Khaled, quickly untying the knots that bound his wrists.

Ghazala lowered herself to the ground, for them to climb onto her back.

'You can't carry us all,' gasped Zayed.

'I can and I will,' she said in a determined voice. 'Just far enough to get us away from the camp.'

Within seconds, they'd all scrambled on to the camel's back, clinging to her and to one another for dear life as she tore across the dunes, with the wind howling behind them. They didn't stop until the pirate camp had vanished from sight and the stars were shining above.

That night, under the silvery glow of the moon, Zayed sat beside his father at the edge of a dune.

'You saved me,' Khaled said, voice low.

'You taught me how, Baba,' Zayed replied. 'And don't forget that I had help from my friends, too.' He felt the comforting warmth of the pearl, now safely back in his woven bag after Charlie had returned it to him.

Exhausted, Max yawned and curled up beside the lamp. 'It's been a long day,' he sighed.

Zayed had already explained to his father about the cat's ability to speak. Luckily, no stranger to the wonders of ancient magic, Khaled had accepted this with no questions.

'But it's not over yet,' continued Max. 'Not until we discover what the lamp *really* does.'

Charlie nodded, staring into its gentle flame. 'We have the pearl. We have the lamp. Now it's time to find the truth.'

And far in the distance, the sand stirred with ancient magic. The city was not finished with them yet.

Chapter 19

The next day, with Khaled and Zayed walking alongside Ghazala, they rode through the dunes beneath a sky washed pale with morning. The wind had dropped, the whispers had faded, and the lamp – now quiet – rested in Jemima's hand. The pearl shimmered in Zayed's palm, its smooth surface reflecting the rosy glow of dawn.

When the sun finally rose over the horizon, the desert turned to gold, bathed in its rays. And beyond the next ridge, Iram of the Pillars, also known as Ubar to some, appeared.

They'd taken a different and very long route across the desert, compared to the way they usually travelled back from the coast... but they were finally home.

A sea of tents and stone shelters stretched across the valley, woven through groves of palm trees and flowering desert shrubs. Children ran barefoot between firepits and wind-towers, and the sound of drums drifted on the breeze.

The moment they were spotted, cries rang out in the camp.

'Zayed! Khaled! They're back at last.'

A surge of people came running out to welcome them — family, friends, and elders.

No one had been expecting the tale of the terrifying ordeal they'd suffered but, after Khaled explained about the pirates' attack, everyone embraced them, rejoicing at their safe return. Zayed was swarmed by cousins, younger brothers and sisters, and his mother, who burst into tears before hugging him close.

'Zayed,' she cried. 'My boy.' Horrified by Khaled's account of what had happened, she realised she might have lost them both.

With tears rolling down his cheeks, he held on to his mother, arms locked tight around her. 'Mama,' was all he said.

Jemima watched with a lump in her throat. She almost envied him this reunion, feeling the depth of their emotion in every hug, every tear, every laugh of relief. It was what she longed for most in the world – to be able to see her own mother again.

The woman looked up and noticed her watching them. Pulling Zayed along with her, she touched Jemima's shoulder. She wore silver bangles that jingled as she moved her arms and had kind eyes that still glistened with unshed tears.

'You are the ones who brought my son home... and my husband too,' she said.

Jemima nodded.

'*Shukran, Habibti* – Thank you, my dear, for helping them,' Zayed's mother said.

Jemima replied with a shy smile. 'We all helped each other.'

But even as the camp was filled with joy at their homecoming, the falcon landed near the children and let out a single cry of warning.

Khaled turned towards the dunes, his face darkening. 'The pirates have followed us,' he said.

And far off, amongst the ruins of the ancient city, dark figures moved across the sand.

'They're coming for the lamp,' said Khaled. 'But I'm not sure if they realise we also have the pearl. Either way, they must be stopped.'

'They'll wait until tonight to launch their attack, try to catch us unprepared,' said one of the elders. 'But we'll be waiting for them – we'll be ready.'

Later, as the desert sun dipped low over the dunes, casting long shadows across the camp, lanterns flickered to life, their golden glow swaying in the soft breeze. The scent of spiced rice and flatbread wafted through the air, but no one was really hungry – not with the threat of pirate blades hanging in the darkness beyond the camp.

The men of the tribe gathered around the campfire to work out a plan. The three children sat cross-legged on the sand next to Zayed and his father. Max had flopped on his side beside Joe and was now snoring loudly.

All eyes were on Zayed as he described how they'd entered the underground city through the Gate of Whispers, telling them what they'd seen and how they'd found the lamp. He also mentioned the bones of the unlucky treasure hunters, recalling the scene with a shudder.

'But there are also things you don't know about yet, Zayed,' said his father. 'Things that I haven't told you about before – you were too young for that burden of knowledge – but I think the time has now come for me to share them with you.'

Zayed frowned. 'What things, Baba?'

'Things like the pearl,' began Khaled.

'I still don't understand,' Zayed said, staring at the enormous pearl cradled in his hands. It shimmered faintly even in the low light. 'Why didn't you tell me what this really was? I thought it was just... the find of a lifetime, a precious gem worth a fortune. I know differently now, though.'

Khaled's weathered face was tired, but his eyes were steady as he looked at his son. 'Because you weren't ready. Because *I* wasn't ready. And because some truths must wait until the moment they matter most.'

He leant forward, his voice low, almost drowned by the crackle of the fire. 'That pearl is not a jewel, Zayed. It's a key. It was kept safe by ancient hands in a time before stories began. It belonged to the Order of the Guardians of the Portal.'

'Is it a portal to... time?' Charlie asked, his brow furrowed. He wondered if Khaled was referring to the same Guardians of Time *they* knew about.

Khaled nodded gravely. 'You've already found out about the gateway buried deep in the lost city – the city hidden beneath the sands, known only to those who keep the old secrets.'

'Yes, and we also know most of what you're telling us,' said Zayed. 'And we saw things down there that I didn't think were possible.'

'So, you understand that it wasn't just treasure the pirates sought,' continued his father.

'It was power – the power to change the past and bend the future. If they unlock the prison beneath the city, they will unleash an ancient evil bound by fire and shadow. An evil that tried once before to rewrite the history of the world.'

Jemima hugged her knees. 'And the lamp? It's part of this, isn't it?'

'Yes,' answered Zayed's father. 'It was created to grant a single wish – one chance to shape destiny. But it was meant as a last resort, not a prize. That is why it was buried. That's why they made sure only one key existed – the pearl. And then the pearl was hidden far below the waves, deep on the seabed, safe from discovery.'

Joe raised his head. 'So how did the pirates find out about it?'

Khaled's jaw clenched. 'They have spies in every port. Treasure-hunters who chase myth and legend, hoping to twist them into weapons.'

Joe looked at Zayed. 'But you found the pearl by accident, didn't you?'

Zayed nodded. '*Hei* -yes, but it was as if it called to me. I had a kind of premonition that day, *yanni* – y'know, and I dived deeper than I ever had before. I still can't believe I survived going so far down.'

'You were meant to,' Khaled said softly. 'The sea chose you. Just as it chose me, long ago. I think the pirates saw you with the pearl on our boat that day, though, Zayed. The captain had a telescope and...'

A horn sounded from one of the sentries on the ridge. It wasn't loud, but it was enough.

'The pirates are coming,' whispered Jemima.

The camp stirred. Men and women rose from their rugs and blankets, gathering weapons, curved blades, bows, and spears. The elders recited ancient words under their breath, lines of protection passed down through generations. The camels were herded into the inner enclosure, and mothers guided their children into the tents for safety.

Zayed grinned despite the tension and slipped the pearl into a carved box his father had given him. 'I'll keep this in here where it's safe.'

'No,' said Khaled. 'We'll *use* it. At dawn, when the moonlight fades, the vault beneath the city will open one final time. If we can reach it before the pirates... we seal it – forever.'

'And what do we do with the lamp?' asked Jemima.

'We must leave it where it was meant to stay,' he replied. 'Locked inside, far from the reach of those who would misuse it.'

Max stood and shook the sand from his fur. 'So, tonight we fight the baddies, defeat evil, and save the world... again.'

Joe laughed, nerves buzzing beneath his skin. 'No pressure then.'

Zayed drew his small, curved dagger and looked to the distant hills, where torchlight was beginning to glow like fireflies. 'Let them come,' he said. 'We're ready.'

Beside him, Khaled rested a firm hand on his son's shoulder. 'They will come. But we will not fail.'

And in the distance, where the stars began to glitter over the dunes, the first shouts of the pirate horde echoed across the desert. Everything would be decided that night.

Chapter 20

Night in Iram of the Pillars wasn't silent. The wind whispered through the ruins. Flames crackled low in clay braziers. Somewhere out in the dunes, a jackal called to the moon.

But something else moved beneath the sand. Something older than the city. Older than memory.

The children sat in Zayed's tent, waiting for him to join them.

He entered quietly. 'My father has sent out scouts. If the pirates come close, we'll lead them into a trap.'

Joe looked up. 'How?'

'The desert hides many things,' said Zayed with an enigmatic smile. 'Come with me.' He motioned for them to follow.

At the edge of the camp, the elders of the tribe gathered around the fallen columns of the ruined city.

As the children approached, the falcon

circled overhead, then swooped low, perching on one of the pillars like a carved statue.

One of the elders stepped forward. He wore a robe the colour of ash and his beard was streaked with grey. He stopped in front of Jemima. 'You are not of this time,' he said, looking directly at her. 'Neither is your cat.'

Jemima blinked, wondering if she'd misheard him. 'Excuse me?'

'He carries a key,' said the elder, pointing to Max's collar. 'It's only given to those chosen by the shadows of time.'

Zayed glanced at Jemima, stunned. 'You didn't tell me he was a *chosen* one.'

'*We* didn't know either,' said Joe. 'Or at least *I* didn't.' He raised his eyebrows as he shot an accusing look at his twin sister.

The elder knelt before the cat. 'That key belonged to the Guardians of Time – keepers of old magic, watchers of the past.' He turned to Joe. 'Your sister has one too. Your arrival here was not an accident. The pirates... they are not just ordinary men, you know. They are *seekers*, hunting for what lies buried beneath Ubar. As Khaled told you, it's not the treasure they seek... not *just* the treasure.' The elder's eyes narrowed. 'What they really want is something more sinister. There is another gateway, one you do not know about, beneath the Pillar of Winds. It was sealed centuries ago, but your cat has the key to open it – or to keep it shut.'

Before any of them could respond, a shout echoed from one of the watch posts at the edge of the camp. 'They're here!'

At once, the tribe burst into action. Warriors readied bows and blades. Fires were snuffed out. Zayed grabbed Joe's arm.

'Come with me,' he said urgently. 'We'll lead them into the trap.'

The group of children ran together into the ruined city, the falcon darting above, screeching a warning. Behind them, pirate riders stormed across the sand on fast horses, faces masked, blades gleaming.

Zayed's father directed the defenders towards the broken arches. 'Fall back to the tunnels! Lead them to the sink traps!'

Zayed and the children ducked through narrow alleys of stone, dodging between leaning columns and fractured statues. The falcon led them to a wide pit covered by palm fronds, loose stone, and a thin layer of sand.

'Here it is,' panted Zayed. 'Now we draw them in.'

Moments later, the first pirate thundered into the ruins.

Max stood tall and raised a paw in the air. He had no idea why he did this, but he saw the ground beneath the pirate shimmer, then collapse, sucking both horse and rider into a hidden chasm.

'Whoa,' he murmured. 'Did *I* do that?'

Zayed stared at the cat in amazement, his jaw dropping open. 'You really *are* part of this, aren't you?'

One by one, more pirates arrived. Some were lost to the traps, but others dismounted, moving more carefully now. One, in particular, cloaked in black, held a curved blade that glowed with a strange energy.

'Their leader, Captain Malik,' whispered Zayed. 'He's not like the others.'

Jemima felt a sudden jolt in her chest, a burning sensation against her skin, as if the golden key on her necklace had recognised the man.

'He's after the gateway,' she said. 'I *felt* it.'

Together, they fled deeper into the abandoned city, until they reached the Pillar of Winds – the tallest structure still standing amongst the ruins. Its pitted, stone surface was etched with ancient script and decorated with spirals that matched the ones in all the carvings they'd seen during their journey through the desert.

As the pirates closed in, the falcon let out a cry unlike any they'd heard before – shrill, ancient, commanding.

The air shifted. The pillar shimmered. And from beneath the sand, a great stone door began to rise, sealed with strange symbols that glowed with the same golden hue as Jemima's key.

'It's the other gateway,' Zayed gasped. 'The one the elder told us about.'

Max stepped forward. 'I think this might be why I'm here.' He didn't know what made him say that or where the words had come from. They just seemed to pop into his head unbidden. He felt the special key on his collar grow hot.

As the cat moved towards it, the stone door fully emerged from the sand with a grinding rumble, revealing an entrance lined with glowing motifs which made a low humming sound. The falcon circled above it, then vanished into the night sky.

Max approached the door, his owl key pulsing with light.

‘It’s opening,’ Charlie whispered. ‘What do we do?’

But the pirate leader, cloaked in black and wielding a menacing, curved blade, stepped forward. His voice echoed strangely, as if not quite human.

‘You don’t understand the power sealed in there,’ he growled. ‘This is no ordinary treasure – this is a portal, a gateway across all of time – past, present and future. And I will be its master. I will control time itself.’

He rushed forward, trying to prise it further open with his bare hands, pushing and pulling at the door. It would not budge.

When she noticed the light on Max’s key, Jemima suddenly sensed what she needed to do. With her heart pounding, she reached under the neck of her tunic and pulled out the key attached to her necklace – it was a perfect match to the one Max wore. With their power combined, the glow of the two golden keys intensified, fusing into a single beam that lit the motifs on the gate.

The pirate lunged, grabbing hold of Max’s key and wrenching it off the cat’s collar. The falcon suddenly reappeared, slamming into Malik’s face and sending him staggering back.

The key dropped to the ground with a metallic clink and rolled away, but there was no time to hunt for it – the door was already opening. Inside was not a chamber, but a whirling vortex of stars and shifting sands – an ancient rift in time.

An elder from the tribe called out urgently, 'Quickly! You must seal it! If that man steps through, he could rewrite history. And he will only use it for evil purposes. He will destroy humanity and our world for all time.'

Max looked at the others. 'We thought we came to save Zayed's people, but maybe we were destined to do this too. Perhaps this was part of it all along.'

'Just do it, Max,' urged Jemima. 'Make the wish. Hurry! Then we'll put the lamp inside.'

Joe grabbed her sleeve. 'Wait. Are you sure? If we do that, we won't be able to use it to take us back home, like Max did.'

'We have no choice,' she replied. 'We have to do this.' She placed the lamp on the floor. 'Come, Max.'

The cat stepped forward with Jemima, both of them facing the portal. Max now knew what he must use his single wish for.

'I wish this gate would close – for good, or

until the time is right for it to open again... when the world is ready.'

Summoned by Max's words, the genie appeared before them.

'Before I grant your wish, Master, you must understand that you will not be able to use the lamp's magic again.'

'I understand,' said Max solemnly. 'This is my wish.'

The genie's voice whispered in the air. 'So it shall be, Master. *As-sam wa t'taa ah* – Your wish is my command.'

Jemima placed the lamp on the floor, pushing it through the opening with her foot.

A loud roar of rushing wind filled the air. The pirates were flung backwards by a gust of glowing sand. With the lamp now inside, the portal sealed itself once more, the whispering voices fading to silence. Captain Malik's blade was wrenched from his grip and clattered to the ground. Powerless, he howled in rage, as he watched the gate vanish back beneath the sand.

'A most wise and selfless decision, for which you have our humble thanks,' said the elder. 'Our tribe is safe, the evil force cannot escape, and the treasure is hidden once more.'

Chapter 21

As dawn broke, peace had returned to the ruins of Iram. The surviving pirates had all scattered and fled. The tribe was safe once more. They rode back through the dunes. The pearl shimmered in Zayed's palm, reflecting the pale pink rays of the rising sun.

In the distance, crumbling towers rose from the dunes. At the edge of the ruins, tents stood like sentinels. Fires flickered. People gathered in silence as they approached, the falcon gliding overhead in a perfect arc.

A sudden shout rang out across the camp. 'Here they come! They're back.'

Jemima, Joe, Charlie, and Max were led towards the great fire pit at the heart of the camp, where the tribal elders gathered, their robes bright in the morning light.

'You have done something no outsider ever has before,' said the eldest, his beard silver and his eyes sharp. 'You entered the hidden city and you returned the lamp.'

Falak perched on a wooden post nearby, silvery feathers gleaming in the sun, watching as Max stretched and proudly bowed his head.

The people laughed.

'You took nothing for yourselves,' continued the elder. 'You did not plunder the riches, buried for so long, as the pirates sought to do. You proved yourselves worthy and pure of heart.'

Jemima smiled. 'We didn't need treasure. It's better left where it is.'

Zayed stood beside her and held out the pearl. 'But we still have... *this*.'

Gasps rippled through the crowd at the sight of the enormous pearl's rosy shimmer. It was magnificent.

'But this is not for selling,' said Zayed. 'Not now, not ever... however much it might be worth. I've discovered that it's far too important to allow it to fall into the wrong hands. It's my duty to keep it safe, to protect not only our people, but the whole world.'

Khaled nodded. 'Well said, my son. Because of you youngsters, the city sleeps safely again. One day, our country will rise and become a home for many. One day, this place – its memory, its knowledge – will help build something greater. An entire nation, perhaps. One rooted in wisdom, not greed, and united in peace.'

A short while later, Max, a little dusty and more thoughtful than before, sat with Jemima, Joe and Charlie, watching the sun rise over Iram of the Pillars.

'D'you think we changed the future?' he asked.

'I think we protected it,' Jemima replied. 'Don't you? We did what we came here to do.'

'It's great when everything works out, isn't it?' said Charlie. 'I mean, when we actually succeed. It doesn't happen every time.'

Joe nodded. He'd been building up to something for a long time and now he just had to get it out. 'Ahem… There's something I want to say, something I *need* to say.' He turned to the cat. 'I'm sorry… for everything, Max. I've been a prat. You were amazing, and I should never have doubted you. Can you forgive me for being so horrible?'

'Forgotten it already,' Max replied. He took a deep breath. 'But just don't do it again… or else!'

They all laughed.

That night, the celebrations began under a smiling crescent moon. There was feasting and dancing, the young girls of the tribe swaying as they swished their long, dark hair to the ancient rhythms of the desert music. The tribe sang songs of victory and survival. Lanterns swung in the breeze. Camels snorted softly. The elders told stories around the campfires.

'Are we going home now it's all over?' Max asked in a low voice.

'I think it's time,' said Jemima. 'There's nothing else for us to do here.'

Joe scratched his head. 'But how? Do we need to go all the way back to the beach where we first arrived? I don't fancy trekking all that way through the desert again.'

'I hadn't thought of that,' said Charlie. 'We usually have to find the exact spot where we landed before we can travel home. What are we going to do? Maybe we shouldn't have put the lamp through the gateway after all.'

Joe turned to Jemima. 'I told you, didn't I?'

Max gave them a worried look. 'The genie sent me home last time, because that was my wish,' he said. 'But if we don't have the lamp any longer, that means we're stuck here, doesn't it?'

Falak clicked his beak. '*La, la* – No, no. You don't need to worry, my friends. It's all taken care of. I've already made arrangements for your departure. At midnight, Ghazala and I will take you to a place where someone will come to send you home.'

When the fire burned low, and the bright stars blinked above, they knew it was time. The children walked with Zayed and his father to the edge of the camp, looking out over the dunes and the ancient ruins of Iram of the Pillars. They stood together, watching as the stars realigned overhead. The wind swirled, and the ground beneath them shimmered with golden light.

'Do you really have to leave?' asked Zayed.

'Yes, we have no choice – we must go home,' said Jemima. 'We don't want our own gateway through time to close and trap us here forever. You found *your* father, Zayed, but don't forget that Joe and I are still looking for *our* parents.'

'I understand and I wish you success,' he replied. '*Yanni* – y'know, you deserve it... especially after everything you've done to help me and my people.'

Khaled placed a hand on each of their shoulders. 'You will always be welcome here. As friends of our tribe. As heroes of Iram.'

'Thank you,' said Jemima. Then she stepped

forward and hugged Zayed tightly.

'You're braver than almost anyone I've ever met,' she whispered.

He smiled, blinking hard. 'So are you.' He pressed a small flower-shaped stone into her hand. 'Take this home with you as a memory of your time in my land.'

'What is it?' she asked, intrigued, feeling the hard edges of its "petals".

'A desert rose – it's a crystal that we find buried under the sand,' he explained.

'Thank you, Zayed. It's so pretty. I'll remember all of this every time I look at it.' She carefully pushed the tiny stone into her pocket.

Zayed turned to Joe and Charlie. 'Thank you for sticking with me. I couldn't have done any of this without you. Your friendship will remain in my heart forever.'

Then, Zayed knelt down and wrapped his arms around Max. 'A special thank you to you, my brave friend,' he said. 'You were a real hero down there, when you made the wish and sealed the gateway. You saved my people. If I hadn't seen all of that for myself, I'd never have believed it. You're the most remarkable cat I'm ever likely to meet in my lifetime.' He rubbed Max's ears.

Max went pink under his fur, glowing at the praise being heaped upon him. 'My pleasure,' he murmured.

'It's time to go now,' said Falak. 'Come, Ghazala will carry you.'

Max leapt up onto Ghazala's back and whispered something in her ear. Beside him, Falak let out a low chuckle. The three friends knew that they would never meet again, but it had been wonderful to renew their acquaintance and work together to defeat evil forces.

Zayed handed Charlie a lantern. 'Take this to light your way, my friends. '*Ma'a salaama*! Go in peace.'

After saying their final goodbyes, and with the camel carrying them on her back, the children and Max turned towards the desert horizon – towards the way home. The falcon flew overhead, guiding them one last time.

As they rode, the moon followed them, casting long silvery shadows across the sand.

And far away, deep beneath the dunes, the city slept again. It might have been lost from sight, but it was no longer forgotten.

'This is the place you must stop, my friends,' said Falak, swooping down to stand beside them as they reached the base of a towering, crescent-shaped dune.

Ghazala knelt down in the sand to allow them to slide off her back.

Jemima flung her arms around the camel's neck. 'Goodbye, dear Ghazala. We'll miss you.'

'Farewell, *Habibti* – my dear,' murmured the camel. 'I'll miss you too.'

Jemima turned to the falcon. 'Bye bye, Falak. Thank you for everything – your bravery, your wisdom and for taking care of us, not to mention saving Max's life the first time he was here.' She dropped a soft kiss on the top of his feathered head. '*Shukran*,' she added shyly.

'*Afwan* – it was my pleasure,' he replied. 'It's been quite an adventure... for all of us.'

Feeling the lantern vibrate in his hands, Charlie placed it on the ground.

The flame inside grew and grew until, with a bright flash of light, the genie from the lamp appeared before them. They didn't understand how Falak had "arranged" this, but they were glad to see him.

The genie turned to Max and bowed deeply. 'The sands have shifted, Master. It is time for you to return home, you and your three companions. I have come to send you on your way and to make sure you travel safely. *Ma'a salaama*! – Farewell. Go in peace!'

Jemima scooped Max into her arms, and the boys held on to her as they waited to be transported forward through time. They took one last look at the desert, knowing they'd left a legacy that would last for generations.

As the world began to spin, a whisper followed them, ringing in their ears as the years flew past, carrying them forward to the 21st century.

'Every choice you make leaves its echoes through time. Be brave, be wise, be kind.'

Chapter 22

'I wish all our journeys home were so quick and painless,' said Jemima. 'None of that awful whirling through the time vortex, feeling as if we're being torn limb from limb.'

The afternoon sun streamed through the window of the upstairs room where their journey had begun and ended. It had become a tradition when they returned from one of their time-travelling adventures to raid the fridge for celebratory snacks, then huddle together and try to figure out what on earth had just happened.

Joe lay sprawled on the rug with his eyes closed. Jemima was curled up beside Max, dusting the sand from the desert rose crystal that Zayed had given her.

Charlie sat cross-legged, clutching his iPad which he'd rushed next door to fetch. He was staring at an announcement for the British Museum's newest exhibition – ***Legends of the Lost City***, decorated with ancient symbols carved on stone pillars, which looked eerily familiar.

'OMG, look at this photo,' he said, pointing at the screen.

In the centre of one of the displays sat an old key and a single feather.

'That's *Max's* key,' squeaked Charlie, holding up his iPad. 'Look at the owl's head on top. When Captain Malik ripped it off his collar, we didn't have time to look for it afterwards.'

'Do you think we could go to the museum and get it back?' the cat asked hopefully. He was devastated that he'd lost it.

'Not a chance,' said Joe. 'Like we could just walk into the British Museum and say one of their exhibits belongs to our cat? In your dreams, pal!'

'Humph! But that's not fair – it's mine,' Max replied, pouting.

'Should have taken better care of it, then, shouldn't you?' said Joe. 'You don't really need it anyway – we still have Jemima's key.'

Max huffed. It wasn't his fault. And if it hadn't been for him, they'd never have been able to shut the portal.

'And what about this?' Charlie zoomed in on the delicate white and silver feather. 'I'm sure that's from Falak's tail. I saw it fall when Max took a flying leap off Ghazala's back.'

Max raised his head with a sleepy sigh. 'It was a *heroic* leap, actually – not a *flying* leap.'

They all laughed. Even now, it was hard to believe they'd really travelled across a desert, outsmarted pirates, and shut a timeless portal that could have unravelled the entire universe.

Jemima held up her small flower-shaped crystal, watching it glint in the sunlight. 'It's weird, isn't it? How history remembers *some* things, but not others.'

'Maybe it's not that it forgets,' Joe said thoughtfully. 'Maybe it just... rewrites it. We closed the portal, locked the lamp away, and left everything how it needed to be. But that key and that feather...'

'Are like fingerprints,' Charlie finished. 'Proof we were there.'

Max let out a long yawn and stretched. 'I'm just glad we didn't have to come back through that time vortex thing again. Honestly, it always feels like my ears are going to end up in a different century from the rest of me.'

Jemima grinned at him. 'I know what you mean.'

For a long moment, they all sat in silence.

Outside, the world was ordinary. Buses rumbled past, birds chirped in the garden, and a delivery van hooted his horn at a cyclist. But inside, each of them carried something extraordinary – memories of courage in the face of darkness, friendship stronger than fear, and a quiet understanding that even the smallest actions could shape the future.

Joe sat up, eyes bright. 'So, what's next?'

'Another adventure, I expect,' Jemima said softly.

Max twitched his tail. 'Hopefully one with fewer scorpions, snakes, and pirates,' he said.

Charlie smiled, slipping the iPad into his backpack. 'Whatever it is... we'll be ready.'

Outside the window, a gust of wind stirred the leaves in the trees. A single feather – white and silver – drifted gently onto the lawn, unnoticed.

But the world noticed. And somewhere, in the quiet hum of time itself, something shifted ever so slightly.

Epilogue

Guardians of Time Headquarters

As the large screen on the wall turned blank, a hush fell over the chamber. For a moment, no one spoke. The spectators had all been holding their breath as the final scene was played out, and they continued to sit in stunned silence when the lights came back on.

'What just happened?' asked one of the guardians, blinking in surprise.

'Something quite extraordinary,' said the Master. 'If we ever had any doubts about our Chosen One, then this has surely dispelled them once and for all.'

'Hear, hear,' said another. 'He certainly rose to the challenge when it counted most.'

'And exceeded all our expectations,' added the Second-in-Command.

The Master turned to Octavius. 'Perhaps now you can understand why I thought it would be a good idea to send our young Chrononauts on this mission?'

'Oh, yes,' replied the junior guardian. 'My goodness, that was exciting.'

The Master inclined his head, with a smile. 'It was indeed.'

'We place a heavy burden on their young shoulders when we send them into situations like this,' said the Second-in-Command. 'I must admit that it does worry me sometimes, what we're putting them through.'

'But it gives me hope for the future,' said another guardian who'd remained silent until that moment. 'Hope that future generations will not let us down. They were faced with a difficult choice but, when it came to it, they didn't wish for power or wealth. Instead, they chose to protect history from those would twist it for their own gain.'

'And they proved the importance of friendship, loyalty, and courage,' said Octavius. 'They really were *so* brave that I wish we could give them a medal or something.'

His earnest remark made the rest of the guardians smile.

The Master nodded. 'Fear not, Octavius. They'll be rewarded... eventually. By the time they've finished, they'll find that their endeavours have not been in vain.'

A flurry of whispers echoed around the chamber, as the guardians chorused their satisfaction at this piece of information.

'This whole episode should remind us of one thing,' continued the Master. 'We should never forget how small actions can influence the future and how the past shapes the present. These are important lessons which humankind is still learning. I think our young time-travellers have just discovered this for themselves.'

The guardians all nodded wisely. They couldn't agree more.

'So, what's next on our list?' asked Octavius. 'Where will we send them in the next chapter?'

'Ah, I have a small job lined up for the Chosen One first,' said the Master. 'And based on what we've just seen, I'm confident that he'll carry out his role admirably.'

See you again soon!
Max

FIND OUT MORE

ABU DHABI AND THE UAE

I'm sure that most of you have heard of Dubai –the second largest of the seven emirates which make up the United Arab Emirates. However, the largest of them is Abu Dhabi which is the capital of the UAE.

Abu Dhabi traces its origins back to the 17th century when the Bani Yas people, a nomadic tribe, first settled in the area around the oasis of Liwa. In the late 1700s, they resettled by the coast to fish and also to dive for pearls, but this was mainly done during the summer months when the sea was clear. Once a fishing village, Abu Dhabi developed into a prosperous emirate, ruled by the Al Nahyan family.

The founding father of the UAE was Sheikh Zayed bin Sultan Al Nahyan who put an end to tribal rivalries, disputes and fighting when, in 1971, he unified the seven separate emirates to form one single nation.

PEARL DIVING

Pearl fishermen operated from traditional wooden boats called Dhows. It was a demanding and dangerous profession. A diver would cover his skin in oil, plug his ears with wax, seal his nostrils with a nose-clip made of turtle shell or animal bone, and wear a woven bag or basket around his neck.

Holding a heavy stone tied to a rope, he would sink down to the seabed. A man on the boat pulled up the stone while the diver gathered oysters and put them in his bag. When his lungs had no more air, he pulled on a line and was hauled back up to the surface.

The history of pearl diving in the UAE goes back to ancient times. The world's oldest natural pearl was found on an island off Abu Dhabi. It was proved to date to around 5800 BC and showed that pearls had been traded in the region since Neolithic times. Pearl trading flourished during the Roman era, and pearls from the UAE have been discovered far and wide across the world, even amongst Viking finds in Scandinavia.

ATLANTIS OF THE SANDS

The Rub' Al Khali desert, also known as the Empty Quarter, is the largest continuous sand desert in the world. It covers 650,000 square kilometres (240,000 square miles) and is filled with enormous dunes. It hides a secret that has fascinated historians, explorers, and treasure-hunters for hundreds of years – a lost city, often called *Atlantis of the Sands*. This legendary place is also known as Ubar, Wabar, or Iram of the Pillars.

Iram of the Pillars was first mentioned in a collection of clay tablets discovered in the ancient city of Ebla, in Syria, dating back to 2500 BC.

Ubar also features in many ancient Arabian legends and appears in the tales of *One Thousand and One Nights* (also known as *The Arabian Knights*). A wealthy city, on the trade routes of desert caravans transporting incense such as Frankincense and Myrrh, spices and other luxury goods, it's thought to have been destroyed by a natural disaster or a divine punishment – a similar fate to that of the legendary city of Atlantis in Greek mythology. Descriptions of Iram of the Pillars, or Ubar, claim that it was built over an enormous underground cavern with a spring that ensured a constant supply of water.

Many travellers and explorers have hoped to find the location of the lost city over the years, including a famous British army officer, diplomat, archaeologist, and writer, T. E. Lawrence – better known as *Lawrence of Arabia*. Lawrence was sent to the area during the First World War to act as a liaison between the British government and the Arab tribes. It was Lawrence who first came up with the name *Atlantis of the Sands,* and he planned to return with an expedition to search for it but he died before he was able to carry this out.

Since then, the quest to find Atlantis of the Sands has continued for many years. Several possible locations have been put forward, following various archaeological investigations and excavations. Some even claim to have discovered it. However, the debate goes on as to whether the lost city was ever a real place or just a myth. Atlantis of the Sands may never be found, but the mystery lives on...

THE ARABIAN ORYX

The origin of the mythical unicorn may well have come from the Arabian oryx. This idea even goes as far back as the Ancient Greek philosopher Aristotle, and the Ancient Roman writer and naval commander, Pliny the Elder, who died during the volcanic eruption of Mount Vesuvius in Pompeii. The oryx, a large white antelope, can indeed appear to have only one horn when seen in profile.

The Arabian oryx has a white coat to reflect the rays of the sun so that it can cope more easily with the extreme desert heat, and its wide hooves are perfectly adapted for walking on sand. It can survive for long periods without drinking water because it gets moisture from eating plants that grow in the desert.

I've seen these beautiful animals for myself in the deserts of the United Arab Emirates... even though I've never seen a unicorn there! I'm especially fortunate to have seen the oryx in the wild because they teetered on the brink of extinction for a while, but I'm glad to report that their story has a happy ending.

In 1972, the Arabian oryx was hunted to the point where they were officially declared extinct in the wild. Luckily for the oryx, a number of them had been rescued in the early 1960s and taken to zoos in America, where a breeding programme was set up to save them. It's a heart-warming success story which ended with oryx born in captivity being taken back home and reintroduced into their original habitat.

ONE THOUSAND AND ONE NIGHTS

One Thousand and One Nights, or *Alf Laylah wa-Laylah* (its Arabic title), is a collection of Middle Eastern folktales that were put together over many centuries. Some of the stories may even date back as far as the 9th century. The first English version was published in the early 1700s and is also known as *The Arabian Nights*.

You might have heard of some of the tales from *The Arabian Nights,* such as *Aladdin and the Wonderful Lamp* and *Ali Baba and the Forty Thieves*. These didn't form part of the original Arabic collection but were added to a later version produced by a French translator. Other stories were also added, including *The Seven Voyages of Sinbad the Sailor*.

A FEW SIMPLE PHRASES IN GULF ARABIC

You will have noticed some Arabic words and phrases that I included in the story. They're not written in Arabic script, which is completely different from the English alphabet, but I've spelt them phonetically, which means that you can say them aloud and hear what they sound like. Here they are again, together with a few extras which don't appear in the story:

***Mar**haba* – Hello/welcome!

*As-salaam alai**kum*** – Greetings! Peace be upon you.

*Wa alai**kum** as-sa**laam*** – response to the above greeting

***Shuk**ran* – Thank you

***Af**wan* – You're welcome (in response to *Shukran*)

*In**shall**ah* – Hopefully/God willing

Ma’a sa**laa**ma – Goodbye

Hei – Yes

La – No

***Yan**ni* – used as a filler in the same way that we say “Y’know/like…” in between sentences in everyday spoken English.

*Hal**ass*** – Enough/done/finished

***Yall**a* – Come on/let’s go

Shway shway – Slowly, slowly/little by little

Ha**bi**bi – Dear/Darling (male)
Ha**bib**ti –Dear/Darling (female)

Baba – Dad

Don't miss Max's solo adventures... The series now continues with the feline hero's next special mission.

MAX and CHARLIE'S HIGHLAND ADVENTURE

SHADOWS OF THE PAST
Book 19

MAX'S HIGHLAND ADVENTURE

When Max the Tonkinese cat is sent on another special mission into the past by the Guardians of Time, he's joined by a companion – the twins' friend Charlie.

Landing in the misty Scottish Highlands of 1746, they encounter Bonnie Prince Charlie – a royal fugitive fighting to reclaim his throne – and agree to help him. With the fateful Battle of Culloden looming, can the courageous pair alter the course of history? Join them for a heart-pounding race through time in this unforgettable tale of bravery and friendship!

If you have enjoyed reading *The Shadow of the Shifting Sands,* or any of the other books in the *SHADOWS OF THE PAST* series, please take a few moments of your time to visit www.amazon.co.uk or www.amazon.com and leave a review. I always appreciate your feedback.

With many thanks,
Wendy

www.ingramcontent.com/pod-product-compliance
Ingram Content Group UK Ltd.
Pitfield, Milton Keynes, MK11 3LW, UK
UKHW040249020825
7199UKWH00002B/122

9 781912 513116